Touching Spirit: Th

James C Washburn

Touching Spirit: The Letters of Minominike

Kal-Ba Publishing
1305 W 7th St
Tempe, AZ 85281

www.kal-ba.com

Front Cover: Photo of *Agoyo-Tsa (Star White),* taken in 1905, was graciously donated by the Charles Deering McCormick Library, *Edward S. Curtis Special Collection*, Northwestern University Library, Evanston, IL

'Moon' Illustrations by: Dave Knapp & Kevin Reinert *luckyraventattoo.com*

ISBN: 978-0692298022

For Margie

Reviews and Endorsements

"This work reveals the spirit of the original free and independent peoples — the roots of our homeland. *Touching Spirit: The Letters of Minominike* accurately reflects our connection to Spirit and deep love of the land. Using values that transcend the separation and division we see in today's world, this book inspires one to join the Original Peoples who lead in helping to unite humanity and bring us all closer to the land."

— **Dave Courchene** — Nii Ganni Aki Inini — First Nations Messenger — Earth Summit, Rio / Human and Ecological Security, Manila / World Peace Summit, U.N. / G8 Summit, Winnipeg / Spokes-person for the movie ***Bridgewalkers***; Recipient of National Aboriginal Achievement Award; Twice co-speaker with Dalai Lama, USA & Mexico

"Read, taste, enjoy this wisdom and be encouraged in the ways of love and faith. People often need a different language to understand and appreciate their own traditions and experience. That is exactly what Pep Washburn has done in this work."

—**Fr. Richard Rohr O.F.M** — Founder of Center for Action and Contemplation/The Rohr Institute; globally recognized teacher of Christian Mysticism Perennial Tradition. Author of 25-plus books including *Falling Upward, Naked Now, Everything Belongs* and *Immortal Diamond*

"Called by many names in the world's wisdom traditions, *Touching Spirit: The Letters of Minominike*, is a powerful reminder that the Spirit within guides each of us in language unique to our individual heart and soul. James "Pep" Washburn is a conduit for the realization of our shared humanity and our shared desire to journey home and discover our Original Face. This book is accompanied with a warning: Your beliefs may shape shift in such a way that causes your life to never again be the same."

—**Michael Bernard Beckwith** — Founder of Agape International Spiritual Center; author of *Life Visioning, The Answer is You, Inspirations of the Heart*, and *A Manifesto of Peace*. Featured on ***The Oprah Winfrey Show***, ***Larry King Live***, ***Dr. Oz***, ***The Secret***

❧❧❧❧❧❧

"This book should be mandatory reading for all. I hardily endorse this work and its message."

—**Dennis Banks**—Naawakamig — Ojibwa Activist; Co-founder of AIM (American Indian Movement); Author *of Ojibwa Warrior*, Actor: ***Last of the Mohicans***, ***War Party***, and ***Thunderheart***

❧❧❧❧❧❧

"Life is not so much about learning as it is about remembering what we already know. In *Touching Spirit: The Letters of Minominike*, the 'Teacher Within' reminds us of this powerful truth and inspires us to note who we already are. The 'Teacher Within' reconnects and reconciles our authentic selves; an experience reading this book will greatly enhance. I am honored to endorse this brilliant literary work."

—**Carlton Pearson** — Author of *God is Not a Christian, Nor a Jew, Muslim, Hindu …* and *The Gospel of Inclusion*; Founder & Spiritual Director of New Dimensions; Chicago

ॐॐॐॐॐ

"The content of these letters are the manifestation of the path the author walks. Beautifully written as seen through the eyes of a beautiful human being. You'll be wanting more!"

—**Dan Hull** — Songide Makwa — Anishnabe Ceremonial Intercessor; Drum Chief; Spiritual Advisor for WI. Dept. of Social Services; Yearly Presenter at Eagle/Condor Foundation Midwest Shamanic Gathering

ॐॐॐॐॐ

"*Touching Spirit: The Letters of Minominike*, is at once evocative and educational. Above all, it demonstrates that people of all cultures long to know and experience the great and good 'Spirit'. I was amazed at the self-revelation of the Creator in everyday encounters with nature. Listen to this aging Native American instruct his adopted grandson: 'A circle, like the Creator, is the shape of perfection, completeness, harmony, oneness. He is all in all — the light of the world is the love of the Creator, which is perfect and complete. It is not broken in pieces to be given a little here, a little there, or none over there…' Gripping from first page to last, I'm proud to give this enlightening work my highest approval. Author James Washburn has struck gold."

—**Ivan Rogers** — President: Good Report Ministries; author of *Dropping Hell and Embracing Grace* and *Judas Iscariot Revisited*

❧❦❧❦❧❦❦

"Through these words, somewhere deep within myself, a knowing was awakened to my oneness with all creation. Do yourself a favor and experience the embrace of our Creator in the pages of this book."

—**Jenny Murphy** — Spiritual Director and Teacher

❧❦❧❦❧❦❦

"A banquet of wisdom for the hungry soul; a river of light for the thirsty spirit."

—**Stanley A. Canfield** — Sojourner on the path that leads us home.

❧❦❧❦❧❦❦

"I keep this book by my bed. When I need to put my heart at rest or center my thoughts on what is real and unchanging, I pick up these 'letters' and peace surrounds me."

—**J. Timut Awa Qamukaq-Washburn** (Quviagijaujuq) — Inuk (Iglulik Group)

❧❦❧❦❧❦❦

"Here are words in tune with the spirit that lies within us and which makes us one. A clarion call to the beauty and power of the love that surrounds us."

—**Glenn Klein** — Author & Host of *Glenn Klein Online*

❧❧❧❧❧

"This work is a great service to the world's seeking community. We are reminded, in spite of voices that would tell us otherwise, that we are forever loved, always have been, always will be."

—**LeRoy J. Bayerl** — Artist traveling by heart

❧❧❧❧❧

"Become attuned to your true self. Touching Spirit: The Letters of Minominike takes you on a journey to look within in order to look beyond."

—**J. E. Vokoun** — Professor, Kendall College of Arts & Science, University of Tulsa

❧❧❧❧❧

"Never discount the power of a simple tongue revealing truth in down-to-earth ways. Read this book and hear creation's still small voice of love."

—**Elizabeth Bye** — Gisiss Winebasige Quae

❧❧❧❧❧

"Reading, I was gently escorted on a journey to the 'Teacher Within', a place of beauty, where we are touched by the Spirit."

—**Jean Abreu** — Wabaningosi Ikwe

"A beautiful inspiring story of life lived close to the Earth and in tune with the Spirit. I endorse this visionary work."

—**Winona LaDuke** — Founder of Honor the Earth; Green Party vice-presidential candidate '96 & '00 ; *TIME* magazine selection - Most Promising Leader; *Ms.* magazine - Woman of the Year; Reebok Human Rights Award; National Women's Hall of Fame 2007

A Word of Thanks

We are often unaware of the significant influence our lives have on others. I would like to thank those listed below who, in no small way, inspired the words of this book.

Michael Paul Mason

David Duncan Williams

Glenn Scott — *Ma'iingan* (Wolf)

Tom Johnson — *Madwebagassin* (Spirit Wind in Leaves)

John "Dusty" Martin — *Naaniibwi Shkweyaang* (Stands In Back)

Alan Christensen — *Mokasiya* (Walks Gently With Open Heart)

Timut Taliruqtalik Qamukaq

Sabina Pauktut Qamukaq

William Aluluuq Qamukaq

Aaron M. Vokoun

Dan Orienti

Kailapi Awa James Orienti

Willis Crowder — *Wakaja Xunuikga* (Young Thunder)

Barb Cain — *Ozaawaa Kinew Quae* (Brown Eagle Women)

John Moore — *Nee Ne Wig Shi Paw Mis Mi Tig* (Standing Tall Tree)

Rod Parkinson — *Sipikkusiw Ma'iingan* (Gray Wolf)

Joey Ann Orienti

Richard Orienti

Lewis Wisniewski—*Bashwakwam Kinew* (Eagle Thunder)

Mark Roberts — *Chii Ode Ininii* (Big Hearted Man)

Diane Champlin-Miller-Ozhaawashkwe Ahnung Quay(Blue Star Woman)

Dave Knapp- *Wassawad Kamig Bishiki* (Buffalo Stands Alone in Field)

Nicole Knapp — *Waabishkozi Makwa Ikwe* (White Bear Woman)

Mary E. Murray

Mike Williams

Jeff Robertson

Cheryl Agen-*NiiMii Shipeg Miigan Ikwe*(Dancing Grey Wolf Woman)

Katherine Borkenhagen -*Nashaka Makwa (She Bear-Talks with Plants)*

Svetlana Myaskovskaya -*Waabishki Mishtite Ikwe* (White Horse Spirit Woman)

Suzan Smith-Davis - *Bashwakwam Bizhiki Ozaawi Makwa* (Thunder Buffalo-Brown Bear)

Karen Yonkers — *Kinew Noodin Ikwe* (Eagle Wind Women)

Ruth Girard — *Niiyo Noodin Ikwe* (Four Winds Woman)

Peepeelee Pijamini

Larry Audlaluk

Illustrations by: Dave Knapp & Kevin Reinert luckyraventattoo.com

Note to Reader

The letters contained in this book are not to be understood as the philosophy, cosmology or belief system of all the North American Native Peoples. They portray the understanding of one individual and are not meant to be a guide to the ways of the aboriginal peoples. The letters reveal insights into truth that is transcendent and cuts across religious systems and ethnic circles. The author of the letters draws from both Christian and native spirituality. He reads the revelation of the Great Mystery in creation and hears the voice in his heart. He does not promote a religious system to be a part of life but rather he demonstrates the total incorporation of spirituality into life. From the past he speaks to us as one who 'looks within' to 'look beyond' in order to behold the glorious and inspiring truth of our fundamental harmony and oneness with creation, the human family and our Creator.

Table of Contents

Map — The World of Minominike

The World of Minominike

Chapter One: Rediscovery

Thirty years of dust covered the small wooden box in the loft. A box I dimly remember carrying from Grandfather's cabin. The box sat atop an ancient rolled up hide of a black bear that encased a number of ceremonial items. My father, James, had recently passed on and I, his adopted and only child, was going through what remained of his eighty-one years of life. His cabin held a random collection of practical necessities along with dozens of nostalgic items. Porcelain utensils, threadbare clothes, Hudson Bay blankets and old flannel sheets, an oiled rifle with cracked stock and munitions, tarnished binoculars. He hadn't acquired much since the passing of my mother, Peepeelee, nearly three decades earlier. My father lived most of those years alone, two kilometers from the reserve settlement of Brochet on the north end of Reindeer Lake.

The old box held letters, brittle yellow-brown with age, and a small fragile birch-bark container. Its lid was sewn with porcupine quills in the design of two ravens. The little case held a downy feather from a goose and six small stones. After my birth parents drown in the lake while ice fishing in the spring of 1928, James and Peepeelee had taken me in. I was only a few months old. Other than the man at the store, a teacher at the school, a local Scandinavian trapper and the priest, my birth parents had been the only whites in the settlement. No photos remain or for that matter may never have existed.

James, of Ojibwa/Cree decent, had married Peepeelee (Bright One) almost twenty years before my birth. They had no children. She was a descendent of the Iglulik and Caribou Inuit in the far north. James and Peepeelee had a mixed marriage that early on caused some talk among the people of northern Reindeer Lake. Indian and Inuit had little to do with each other, ignorance, misunderstanding and superstition being the cause.

Fourteen winters after my adoption I was attending school in Winnipeg, 700 kilometers south, when Peepeelee passed on. It was mid-

September. The school master, a soft looking round man with tiny glasses, graying goatee and breath that smelled like hand rolled cigarettes, sent me home on one of the shallow draft York boats that still worked Lake Winnipeg during the War.

The Saskatchewan River flows into Lake Winnipeg from the west and spills over a series of terraces near the diminished settlement of Grand Rapids. Upon arriving at Grand Rapids I was picked up by a Chipewyan man and his family. I traveled with them on the Saskatchewan and smaller rivers northwest to Pelican Narrows. A plane regularly flew from there to Brochet on Reindeer Lake. The pilot took me home without charge after hearing about my mother, Peepeelee, passing on. My arrival lightened our sorrow, but resulted in my skipping the rest of that school year.

It was during that winter that my father, James, retrieved the box of letters in the cabin's loft. I was intrigued that they were addressed to me, and although I read several they had little meaning at that stage of my life. All were from James' grandfather, born in the early 1850s. His ancestors migrated into the Reindeer region from the south and east. He went by the Anishnabe name of Minominike Gissis Makwa—Rice Moon Bear. (mĭ nö mĭ nĭ kay gē zĕs mă quă)

As I looked over the letters at that time of my life, and being fascinated by the fact that every letter was addressed to me, images of this aged man started coming back. He had been so deeply interested in this white boy that he had written me dozens of letters over the course of several years before departing from this world. I was going on seven when he left. I recall a broad shouldered straight-standing man with large rough hands and two long braids of gray hair. He would keep me warm inside his coarse canvas jacket, holding me next to his heart. He smelled of black spruce wood smoke and beaver tallow from his trapping. His voice was quiet and deep. I was always happy in his presence. After reading several letters, I had closed up the box and returned it to the loft. There it remained, not to be opened again until this day following my father's death three decades later. The letters took me back over many snows.

Brochet has been a settlement for over 150 years. Missionaries came to the Reindeer Lake region in the mid-nineteenth century. The lake straddles the northern border between Manitoba and Saskatchewan. Settlers built a church, offered a source of supplies for the people, and over time the settlement grew. Grandfather Minominike Gissis Makwa had attended the mission school during the 1860's. He completed a number of grades and was sent away to seminary. My father, James, told me that apparently Minominike was brilliant and insightful. Church authorities had intended that he someday be among the first ordained natives in Canada. He went on to tell me how, after some years of learning at the seminary, Minominike could not endure the torment between heart and mind. His heart was speaking one thing while his mind was being schooled in another. He left the seminary and returned to the birch, spruce and tamarack of the Reindeer region to reconcile the two voices.

Minominike married a girl named Adik, which means Caribou. I faintly recall the setting of their cabin along the Cochrane River east of Brochet. He fished, trapped and raised a small family. Only one of his children survived childhood, and from that child, Pembina, my adoptive father James was born. It was a life surrounded by the quiet of the north—a good place to think about things of the Spirit.

Minominike Gissis Makwa, Rice Moon Bear, was a spiritual name. During the late summer and into fall, when the wild rice is ready for harvest, makwa (bear) has been eagerly eating his fill of all he can find. An unseen force drives makwa to prepare for his great winter sleep. So, too, with this man and his insatiable hunger for things of the Spirit. His letters spoke of a life filled with understanding and peace, a life ready for the great rest. I sensed a spirit in touch with the Creator and one with the world, yet possessed with the urgency of a high calling.

Now three decades later, unlike when I was the boy of fourteen, the letters spoke with a surprisingly clear voice. My mind was being challenged— no, shaken—and renewed by ideas not entirely comfortable in light of my imposed worldview and education. Although I had attended the same school and gone away to the same seminary as he, I had not committed to resolve the conflict between my heart and the teachings poured into my mind. I assumed the school and seminary teachers knew best. As I read his letters, a sense of inner agreement rose up in my heart. At the same time, my indoctrinated mind challenged the words. I imagined this to be similar to the experience of young Minominike. Deep inside, a secret chamber of awareness was being warmly opened like a drawer that had always been there but remained closed.

The light outside grew dim. In early summer, at fifty-eight degrees north latitude, this angle of light hinted at the approach of midnight. The letters had captured me for nearly five hours. I had been absorbed in their voice. Time was meaningless as this old man, rising up from the past, spoke his words.

I pulled a wooden match from a tin box and reached to light the kerosene lantern on the table. The match sparked an urge to walk the shoreline not far from our old cabin's porch. Soon my feet set up a clatter as I strolled over the stones along the shore. Yellow tinged wisps of clouds were reflected on the lake's black mirror surface. A lake trout broke the stillness, distorting the water as far as I could see in the twilight. The letters of Minominike rippled through my presumed certainties.

Chapter Two: Minominike, Peepeelee, James

The early light woke me after only a few hours sleep. I had had a room to myself in our old cabin as a child. My father, James, built this log addition of black spruce and tamarack when I came to live with him and Peepeelee. When fear stalked my young mind, this was my haven, my sanctuary. Last night I had once again crawled onto my former resting place, a bed of ropes stretched over a frame of shaved birch covered with the same thin mattress of my youth. Now, as I sat up, anticipation for the new day rose in my chest. I hadn't sensed such eagerness in years. I was hungry to get back to reading and pondering more of the letters that had slept for so long in the loft.

Old words on yellowed paper brought to life a man of faith who embraced all that his many years had granted. Joy and sadness, life and death, riches and poverty—all received with gratitude. It seems clear to me that a supernatural humility lay at the center of his being. No matter what life dealt him, whether understood or not, he maintained a tranquil sense of being looked after and cared for. He seemed possessed of a holy carelessness, allowing him freedom to receive and live each day.

It was obvious from his teachings and life story that simplicity allowed his voice to be clear. Though much of his life would be considered harsh by today's standards, the distraction and clutter of too many things might easily have muted his tongue with wordy shallowness. His letters were anything but shallow. Great truths are essentially simple and their expression need not be complex. Pondering these things, I stretched my back to meet the day.

Some letters seemed to have been exposed to drops of water. The ink being diluted, diffused and spattered. This always seemed to occur on letters of a clearly impassionate tone and deep caring. I imagined this old man writing in the long darkness of the northern winters under warm kerosene light, tears falling onto his pages of water based ink. His words were like his large rough hands again taking me into the canvas of his coat. There, my ear on his chest, his heart was clearly heard.

My thoughts turned to my mother, Peepeelee. She had seemed especially fond of Minominike Gissis Makwa. Being Inuit, she had left her family behind in the far north a few years after marrying James. Minominike became her substitute father/grandfather. I recall them laughing often together, sometimes so hard they cried.

Peepeelee was frequently ill. This illness eventually took her life. She was in her early 50s. When she was not well, she would ask my father to ask Grandmother Adik if it was okay for Minominike to come for a stay. His presence was good medicine and always lifted her. There were times when pain caused her to be despondent and I remember them sitting together on the porch or near the woodstove, his hands holding hers. Little conversation passed between them during those times.

Had I known my birth parents I would have wanted them to be just like James and Peepeelee. There was never any doubt about my unconditional acceptance in their cabin. My adoption was not a legal affair. In those days it was not considered necessary. There are no orphans among the people. There are many fathers and mothers to go around. Very likely there was little discussion about my needs or the willingness and desire of James and Peepeelee to take me into their cabin. My birth parents were taken. James and Peepeelee, married many years, had an abundance of love to give. I was in need. End of story. The few whites in Brochet at the time also knew it was god.

Until going south to Winnipeg for secondary schooling, I loved life in the cabin of these two wonderful people. It is hard for the north, or any remote settlement for that matter, to compete with the allure and trappings of the white world. James and Peepeelee knew this. Because of my whiteness and the world to the south, I would all too soon be leaving them. It was in that first year of my secondary schooling in the south that Peepeelee died. As I look back on it, my absence may have been too much added on top of her poor health. Be that as it may, in only a few short weeks of my leaving, her Being departed.

Thus, I came home and stayed the winter with James, saw the letters that first time and continued my education the following year. The day I departed by boat for Southend and on to school, his conversation was broken, his eyes avoiding mine so I would not see their frequent tears. James was in his early fifties at the time and he would spend the next thirty years virtually alone. I returned for a couple months each summer over the next few years, and for visits at Christmas and Easter. After graduation it was on to seminary and my trips home were reduced to a few two-week stays each year.

Peepeelee and I had been his life. James was happy, though lonely. He continued guiding for the few hunters and fishermen who ventured that far north until his legs prevented him from easily getting around. Government assistance helped and the church at Brochet looked after him now and then. He would always attempt to be stoic about my leaving when my visits were over. With watering red eyes he would turn quickly from the dock for the hour walk back to our cabin near the shoreline. He kept his face turned away until my boat or plane was far out on the lake. I would see him slowly raise and hold his left arm, the one closest to his heart, high and straight into the air.

James had read the letters that Minominike wrote to me. He understood and treasured their significance. I had discovered a small note from him in the old wooden box. It said simply, "Grandfather has much truth to say. Listen to his words with your inner man. They are good and can heal the world."

Chapter Three: Tulugaq Kagagi

It was Minominike Gissis Makwa who gave me the name Tulugaq Kagagi. James and Peepeelee said he'd chosen this name for several reasons. First, Peepeelee was Inuit, thus the Inuk name for Raven— Tulugaq. James was Ojibwa/Cree, thus Kagagi, also for Raven. Tulugaq Kagagi is literally "Raven" in the two tongues. Being of white origin in a native home also meant I would be of two worlds. And, because ravens are never alone, it was his way of teaching me that I would never be alone either.

Minominike said there would come a day when I would go through considerable change in how I saw the world. The Raven is a symbol of change. Little did I realize his letters would be the catalyst for my profound change in worldview and who I thought I was.

The school at Brochet was a mission school. Almost every year brought a new teacher, sometimes two in the same year. It was difficult for these teachers to come north into such remoteness. Even when they felt they were called to train up the young of the north in the ways of the southern white world and teach them the Bible, the isolation was often too much. It was also difficult for a dedicated teacher, expecting to see her students every day, have them show up only haphazardly. Attendance was disheartening.

A school day consisted of the usual reading, writing, arithmetic, Bible, geography and history classes. These were, of course, punctuated with keeping the wood stove going, recess if outside temperatures wouldn't produce frostbite in less than twenty seconds, tutoring or being tutored by other students, visiting the outhouse and general mischief. We perfected the art of spit wad warfare and note passing and every instructor was tormented until repartee was established. All grade levels, never a total of more than thirty plus students, participated in Bible class together. This was the one subject during which discipline was never an issue. We knew, after our prayer to start the class, that God was watching. Should our memories fail, Miss Dunn, Miss Callahan, Miss

Zable and numerous other teachers would swiftly remind us of His displeasure and wrath. At times, a meter stick assisted our memory.

James and Peepeelee took great interest in what I was learning and rarely spoke contrary to my training. There were times, however, when I sensed through the questioning look on their faces, that they were opposed to some of the ideas. To avoid confusion in my mind or conflict with the mission, they would speak in quieter tones between themselves. A few times I recalled them talking to Minominike regarding these things. I was not particularly interested, though I do recall one such evening. After being set on his lap, Minominike encouraged me to listen to the "Teacher Within" as much as to my teachers and elders "without." He then burned a small amount of cedar and using his eagle feather, fanned the smoke over me. He said all would be well and I went back to pestering one of our hairy dogs. All in all, I liked my six years of school in Brochet. I especially enjoyed Bible classes and yearned for more.

Minominike passed on when I was seven years old. I was told he had gone to be with Grandmother Adik who had left this life five or six years after I'd come to live with James and Peepeelee. Minominike missed her very much. I do not recall seeing Grandfather's body when he died. It was as though he simply walked across the stone beach into the trees and onto another world. At his passing we visited his cabin on the Cochrane River to retrieve some of his things. While there James kindled a fire on the sand bank overlooking the tannin-stained water. Through a long drizzle, and in spite of a heavy bug hatch, he tended the fire for four days. He never left it and Peepeelee and I often sat with him in silence. Now and then James whispered a prayer of thanks. At the end of the four days, we told Minominike Gissis Makwa he was free to leave on his journey to be with the Creator of All Things.

Minominike gone, I cradled only his small wooden box of letters on our slow walk home. I was told these were his gift to me and someday, through them, I would again hear his voice. I placed the box in the loft and began to realize how much this man had been a part of my Being. At night, in my birch and rope bed, I felt the void of his departure and wondered if he missed me too. Sometimes Peepeelee heard me crying and came into my room to rest her hand over my heart.

My friends and I never lacked ideas for adventure and play. Only for a few weeks during the summer was it warm enough for us to actually swim in the lake. We had our dogs to run with and in the winter they pulled us around on toboggans. It seemed the presence of Minominike was forever near no matter what the day had in store. His image was never far from my mind and I truly missed him.

He had often told me about our relations, the animals, and their habits, and encouraged me to listen to their voices. Maybe, he said, they were calling my attention to something the Creator wanted to tell me. He instilled a deep respect for this world formed "without the hands of men." Everywhere, he pointed out, the voice of the Creator was being spoken. This temple, as he referred to the world, was endlessly singing of joy, life, trust, goodness and unending love. All that was, was good, and my life was filled with anticipation for each new day.

I had often played a game with him. He said that Raven, the scruffy black bird of the north, is never alone. He was, of course, instilling in me that I, Tulugaq Kagagi, was also never alone. However, I took it as my job to prove him wrong! Somewhere, somehow I would find a lone Raven. Week after week, month after month, I pointed out what I thought was a solitary Raven. To my wonderment and frustration, I never did win this game, though it was a lesson I often failed to remember as time went on.

Minominike taught that wisdom for life was already waiting in our hearts, needing only to be heard. We simply had to center down, look within, listen, and the Teacher's voice would quietly speak. He said it was easy to be distracted from hearing His word living inside us. Though Minominike's wisdom told me that much of what I would be seeking to learn later in life was already present in my heart, I continued to feel drawn to formal schooling. A year after graduating from sixth grade, I talked my parents into asking the mission to extend my education.

That first year in secondary school in Winnipeg was, as I mentioned, cut short by Peepeelee's passing. My desire to return to school in Winnipeg or to continue staying with my father, James, produced an inner tension. James understood this and after that winter, despite his broken heart, encouraged me to go south. Returning to school in Winnipeg, I developed an even greater desire to learn. Three years later, I enrolled in seminary and was on track for ordination. Following a number of years serving as an assistant in several parishes, I assumed the pastorate of a large church in America. My upward career path was exciting and gave me an inner feeling of importance. It was there I stayed until returning upon James' death, and spied the stained and dust-laden box in our loft and rediscovered the letters of Minominike.

Chapter Four: Voice of Minominike

Minominike's letters carried his voice. I found great comfort in the way he spoke through the letters. He often left his intended meaning to the reader to discover on his own. He would never intrude with demanding explanation. "It is for each person to learn," frequently ended his letters. It was pleasant to hear this voice. Although his writings were not always grammatically correct, he was articulate.

As the black flies trapped in the cabin searched for freedom near the window frames, I began to ponder the arrangement of his extraordinary teachings. Each was rolled and tied with red string. Numerous letters were bundled into groups and also tied with the same red string. It appeared that each bundle danced loosely around a common theme, a mystical organization that spoke of hidden levels of understanding. Some letters referred to a happening in his life. Some also contained a word from Grandmother Adik written by Minominike's hand, as Adik could neither read nor write. Sometimes he would comment on a recent event or a person we both knew. At times I could not remember the event, but his point was clear none-the-less. From seemingly mundane occurrences, he heard the voice of the Spirit revealed. As he wrote over the course of several years, the letters deepened. Although the mystical and mundane are interwoven, it was as though he was walking me into sacred life, every letter and story, an allegory calling me to experience living in the divine. First with a voice as if speaking to a child, then with more mature word pictures and finally speaking almost as a mystic—one who looks within to look beyond.

As I finished the final bundle, a single letter remained at the bottom of the box along with a paper folded into a pouch. The pouch contained tobacco as an offering. This final letter was not held together by red string but rather with two fine sinew cords. One died green and the other blue, the colors of earth and sky. His handwriting appeared unsteady as if trembling, different than the others. I am certain he knew the end of his days had come and it was finally clear to me why I didn't remember seeing his body.

I reproduce here the letters of Minominike as he wrote them. To honor his voice, I have not corrected grammar or changed his words in any way other than taking the liberty to correct spelling. I have also translated Anishnabe words or phrases used to indicate the moon in which the letter was written, the name of an animal or other items. He would, at times, alternate between English and his native dialect. The letters need no interpretation or justification. They speak for themselves. In Minominike's language the letters are 'midewiwin' which can be translated as 'The Way of the Heart.' Read and listen. Perhaps the Teacher may again be heard in your heart as in mine. Perhaps not. No matter. If not in this life, then clearly in the next you will know that no one is ever alone. Eternal Spirit is here. Always was. Always will be. The teaching of the ravens is your truth, too.

Letters One through Six

Ode'imini Giizis

Letter One
1 —Ode'imini Giizis 1931
(Time For Picking Berries Moon)

Tulugaq Kagagi —
    I am Mishomis (Grandfather). It is a good
thing to have you in the family to be with us.
Your new father and mother are happy. You are
the only one they have. You are very small and
my years may be few left so I am told to write and
someday you will understand my words. They are
words coming from Spirit who teaches me and
will teach you too. Spirit can bring you to be
satisfied with life. This is for you and each person
to learn.

    You are almost three years with us now.
Nokomis (Grandmother) Adik holds you when she
can but her arms are not strong. It is hard for
her to breathe and maybe you will not remember
her. She knows I have been told to write and she
sends her words to you too. I will write them.

    - — . — .
        Hello little Tulugaq Kagagi. You are a
beautiful boy. I love you like your mama and
papa. You have a good home. Always listen and
consider words of your parents and elders. We
will pick more berries together soon and you can
eat all of them you want and all the fish and

Wewe (goose) too. I love you ...Nokomis Adik
(Grandmother Cariboo)

- —· —·

Grandmother Adik enjoys picking berries with
you very much, even though you eat them fast as
you pick.

First I tell you a little about Adik. She is a
beautiful person. Very kind and takes good care
of me. We have lived in cabin together for almost
60 snows. She was helping missionaries when I
went to their school. She had very long hair and
she had big soft eyes like the Caribou, which is
her name. I went away to the seminary but left in
a few winters and came home. I liked Adik and
married her and we had children. Two were
taken early in life. I will tell you about this in a
letter. This was hard but Adik is like her name.
She kept going like Caribou does on their
migration journey. She kept me going too in the
sorrow. She used to help with the skins from
trapping but her arms and hands have lost
strength and pain her now.

We like very much to walk the riverbank near
our cabin at night with the moon and stars. It is
good to hear the insects and fish in the water
when the wind is quiet. In winter moose follow
the river too and we scare them out of their beds

at night. We have taken you on these walks and you are sleeping when we are done.

Now I will tell you a little of your second parents, James and Peepeelee (Bright One). James is the first son of our last son, Pembina. He is a strong man and gives his life to Peepeelee. He traveled far north on a trip with the missionary when he was young and met Peepeelee. He stayed in the north with missionary for a year. When they came back he missed this Inuit girl. His father, Pembina, didn't know about these Inuit people and said it might be hard, maybe not a good thing to marry her, but James went back with the missionary again and it seemed well with her family. So, that is how she came south to be with us.

All these years they have no children of their own and were sad about that. It happened that your parents drowned in Reindeer Lake in the spring after you were born. James and Peepeelee knew them. Peepeelee helped your first mother at your birth. They drowned just a few moons later after you came into the world and it seemed right to the ininiwok (people) that you should go to their cabin to be with Peepeelee and James. We were all very sad but happy too. Creator always leads us to do the right thing when we look for help. I am sure your white parents too are happy for your life you now have.

James is good at hunting and fishing. He takes out whites from the south to guide them. You would be right to watch him and learn to respect these ways. You will then never be without. The fish, the animals and the birds will give you their bodies to provide for you. This is the **GREAT GIVEAWAY** teaching that the Creator shows us. It is among the highest teaching and understanding. Our animal relations show us His great love in this.

This will end these first words. Adik is calling that it is time to go to bed. Tomorrow is another day to see what is sent our way. I have made a wooden box from cedar to keep these words in. Someday James will give them to you. You will be older at that time and able to read them. You will walk on your path and learn to read with both your mind and your heart and learn to listen to the Teacher within. This is for you to learn.

Love,
Mishomis (Grandfather) Minominike Gissis Makwa (Rice Moon Bear)

Letter Two
2 —Ode'imini Giizis 1931
(Time for Picking Berries Moon)

Tulugaq Kagagi —
   Hello again. It is very late next day. First star is giving light in earth's shadow to the east and sun is set. Moon will come up soon so I am going to tell you the story of how great Kagagi (Raven) redeemed the world from darkness. I have been given this story. Someday you will love this story and it will be the rock to build your life on. I will speak directly in my letters most of the time but sometimes I will tell a story as I am now. There are many traditional stories of the Ininiwok (people) but this is a story that came to me.

   When the world was made, the first man and women and all our relations, the animals, lived in harmony and peace. They did not feel afraid of life or of Creator who had shaped all things. But, a manitou (spirit) came to them and deceived them by saying, some things were to be feared. It said that if they gave it permission to keep the sun, moon and stars all to itself, the manitou (spirit) would show them wisdom of what was good and what was not. The manitou said in this way they could be powerful and have security. So they believed the manitou and soon began to fear things and crave for power and security. Thinking that this would be helpful in making them fill with great knowledge and power they gave this right to the manitou to keep the light of the world.

Quickly the spirit gathered up the stars the moon and sun and took them away. Now the man and women could see only by glimmer of the firefly and glowworm and some small mushrooms. They had been tricked and deceived and now their eyes as well as their minds were in darkness. They stumbled around pretending to see and understand but they were really filled with confusion, fear and insecurity.

Raven could see in the dimmest of light and as he was flying by he saw them in this state, for no matter how low the light, his eyes can see. He had pity on them and asked how it happened they had given away the world's light. After hearing how they fell for the lie Raven said that when the fullness of time came he would retrieve back the sun, stars and moon for the world.

After many years Raven knew the time had come. He flew down to the earth and found a young girl who lived near where the sun, stars and moon were kept by the deceitful manitou in a box of iron. Raven kept his sharp eye on her and one day when she was dipping a drink in a stream he turned into a tiny spruce seed and floated into her cup. With the help of firefly she saw the tiny spruce seed but her heart said not to be afraid of it. So she drank it up with the water.

The spruce seed began to grow and take form as a boy child inside her. When her time came she gave birth. The little boy's eyes were sharp and burned as if filled with fire and light. The boy lived with her in the world's darkness for some years until one day the keeper of the iron box where the sun, moon and stars were kept hidden away, came home. At that moment the boy began to cry with great sorrow. He wept and howled and cried until the owner of the box was upset. He told the girl to make the boy be quiet but she couldn't. Finally the keeper of the box where the sun, moon and stars were kept could stand it no longer. Seeing that the keeper was at the end of his wits the boy pointed up to the box and made gesture to see it. The keeper was cautious to let the boy see the box where he greedily kept the beautiful light locked away. But, he could not withstand the boy's crying anymore.

The boy quieted down when the box was lowered to him. At once he changed back into Raven and grasped the box with his claws, flying into the sky. High into heaven he went making the great circle of the whole world where he released the sun, moon and stars.

Once again the light of the world was shining. Once again there was no time or place, no person or relations who were not under the light of the sun, moon or stars. Raven had redeemed the light with his crying and sorrow and given it back to all the world.

No matter where you go, Tulugaq Kagagi, there is always the light that Raven has given— Misiweshkamagad sagiiwe (all is covered with it). No matter how dark you may think it is around you or around another person, you just have to let the eyes of your heart adjust and you will glimpse the light that Raven sees and has given to us all. Allow the Teacher within to train your eyes to see wherever you are or with who mever you meet. You will then perceive the light of the world is there. Remember, no matter how dim the light, Raven's eyes know it is there and in all people.

This is something for you and each person to learn. Listen to One who speaks within. Think on these things. It is good.

The sun is now gone to bed and the moon and stars are shining. The life of the night is out and I too am tired for bed.

Love,

Mishomis (Grandfather) Minominike Gissis Makwa (Rice Moon Bear)

Letter Three
Aabita Niibino Giizis 1931
(Halfway Through Summer Moon)

Tulugaq Kagagi —

I have been repairing a canoe to work the river in the fall moose hunt. That is why it has been awhile since I wrote the story of Kagagi (Raven) and the light of the world.

I think I will be more direct about this story. Its meaning you already have in your heart since birth but maybe it is hidden from you, so this teaching will unearth it again. I read the last letter to Adik and I was told I should be more direct. She is discerning so I should listen to her. I will explain some things so that the medicine of this teaching can be established strong in your inner person.

I will not retell the story. You can read it again and let it speak.

As humans we think we are not living with the light of life, the Creator's presence. We deceive ourselves or are taught to think that the Great Spirit is displeased with us. We judge ourselves unworthy of His light and so we believe we are living in darkness, but this is the lie. All humans are born with the light of the Creator and it can never be extinguished.

Some nights when you go to sleep you wake up feeling cold and you think the fire in the stove has gone out. You look inside and it seems black and dark. But, when you feed good fuel like dry spruce or cedar down into the dark coals, pretty soon the fire rises up. It is like this with us humans. The Creator's fire within us can never die. He is the Great Mystery and never ending. Can He die? Not in the slightest bit!

He put His Breath of Life into us. This Breath is His Spirit. It is one with the Creator. It is eternal. It is the light. He pitched His tent within us when He saw us in our human mothers and He loves the campsite. He will never leave or forsake His camp and His fire burns without end.

Misiweshkamagad sagiiwe (all is covered with it)—the Love, the Light of Life, the Fire of the Spirit is in all. Some, by the helping grace of the Creator, know this. Some do not. But, the Light of Life, the Fire, the Love, is there whether they know it or not. Some learn and begin to kindle the fire and it burns brightly with much heat and light. Some are distracted or the ashes of life cover their fire and so the light is not so bright. In some it is hidden in their stove with the door shut and cannot be seen. It is not for me, or you, or anyone to judge them. The Creator knows. Someday when the distractions of this life, when their stove door is opened and the ashes covering the fire are removed, then His Light will blaze. This is the way it is with all of us. We all have parts of our Spirit fire covered.

In this world there are many who do not know that they have been loved and given the Spirit. The more you listen to the Voice within teaching you of His presence, the more you will live freely. Then many may see your eyes shine with light like the little boy in the story. This may help them to know the truth of the great light within them too.

That is the noble medicine in the story of how Raven redeemed back the light of the world. You can live free, in greater harmony and peace within your life and with all people when you know this and let it guide you. You know that all people are equal because all are equally gifted with His light and equally loved by Raven. This is the greatest truth. This is the greatest teaching. I think on it every day and let its medicine give me life. Fear runs away and I can see and hear the Creator more clearly. My heart rests and a power lets me be who He made me to be.

What I have written is all for now. Adik says it is good and has helped with the story of Raven and the Light of the World. She also wants me to write in her words now.

Hello my Tulugaq Kagagi. Minominike has written well. This is a truth that is best of all there is to learn in life. Today I helped him get his canoe repaired. Maybe when you come to visit next time we will take a short trip on river and fish. Namegossika (trout) is catching bugs on the surface now so maybe she will let us catch and eat her. If she does we will give thanks for her kindness, roast her with butter from the store at Brochet and eat with tea and some dry strawberries we picked together last moon. I am breathing better now since last we were together. I can't wait to hug you again and hear you laugh.

Love — Nokomis (Grandmother) Adik

Goodnight and love from Mishomis (Grandfather) too.

Minominike Gissis Makwa (Rice Moon Bear)

Letter Four
Manoominike Giizis 1931
(Rice Gathering Moon)

Tulugaq Kagagi —
    This is the moon of my birth. About seventy-nine winters past. Missionaries came to our area just a few snows before my mother gave me life.

    You have just left us a day ago. Peepeelee and James were here for visit of two days. James helped me with fixing the cabin wall with tarpaper. It will be much warmer this winter. They brought some smoked fish. You and Adik played often by the river. Maybe you will remember this visit when you read the letter someday. This is when the makwa (bear) came along the riverbank and you and Adik were startled. Adik jumped and the bear saw you both and tried to run away but fell off into the river and couldn't get up the steep bank. So, she swam to the other side as fast she could. Then making a woofing noise she ran away. She must have thought she was going to be eaten and was not yet willing to give herself away.

    We are laughing about it again. It was hilarious and our sides hurt from laughing.

    You are only three but I think you may remember this someday.

I am going to tell you a little about my life when I was young. It will help you in understanding the teachings. I went to the missionary school in Brochet and learned many interesting things. The teachers thought I was quite intelligent. I was too. I learned things very fast. Better than my friends. All but one of my friends from my class is passed on from this life through the western door. Someday, maybe soon, I will pass on too.

So, I was always getting very good marks and I especially liked to learn about the way of the Spirit. I could hear Spirit's voice inside me when we studied about such things and it filled me with life and great joy every day.

You are like this, Tulugaq Kagagi. I see it in your eyes that Spirit's voice is loud in you and you feel Spirit's presence and embrace.

After five or six years there was no more schooling here. I spent a year with father and mother and then the church leader came to our cabin. He said there was a chance for me to get more education in the south. I thought it would be good and my father and mother thought it over. I was about fourteen winters when I left for school and the seminary. I was there about three years but would come home in summer and sometimes during Christmas or Easter if ice was to be trusted on the lakes.

I was learning more wonderful things but sometimes there were teachings that did not seem right. I loved much of what I learned but these other things did not sit well in my Being. My heart and mind were in conflict. I would hear that many people were not accepted by the Creator. It too was said that many people did not want to know the Creator. But Spirit would tell me differently. The teachers would say that people who were not accepted by the Creator would be in suffering forever after they passed on. They would be left out in the cold and never be with the Creator. I was wounded inside because I knew that the Creator loves all people equally, even those who do not or cannot hear Him at this time in their existence. Why would a loving Father of all people treat some this way?

Do you remember, Tulugaq Kagagi, how in the story of Great Raven the light of the world shines everywhere   on   the   whole   world? Misiweshkamagad sagiiwe (all is covered with it). The great circle of the world is not in pieces. It is unified and there is no breaking the circle because the Creator has made the circle of the world one, as Creator is One. A circle, like the Creator, is the shape of perfection, completeness, harmony, and oneness. He is all in all. The light of the world, which is the love of the Creator, is perfect, complete and it is one. It is not broken in pieces to be given a little here, a little there, or none over there. I was not able to make these contrary teachings reconcile with this clear truth of universal love and have this settled in my heart.

My teachers, who were my elders, and who I respected, were only teaching with half their person. They were teaching with their minds only. They seemed to have let the voice in their heart be shouted down by the voice of the mind.

This is what I mean. Listen closely. When you are born, your heart knows the love and voice of the Spirit and you are in harmony with it. But, it has no human language. Spirit speaks to you the WORD of the Creator but without a worldly tongue. It has a form but not a worldly speech. It has conversation with your Being but not with sound. Now, when you grow older you learn other words made of sounds that come from the world. You store them in your mind. You develop a language with them to sort out life and to understand this world. Soon the voice of the mind becomes louder and you begin to listen to the words of this worldly tongue more and more and give it greater importance. This may be at the expense of the WORD that comes from eternity, inside the center of your heart. After a while, with so many people, they think the only way to know things is with the word in their minds. So the WORD of the Creator in their heart gets pushed to the side where He waits for the fullness of time to be heard again. Many people, maybe most, are not in harmony.

For many the mind is too loud and they are distracted by unbalanced worldly teachings and indoctrination or by their misunderstanding of happenings in life. Yet, if they quietly look and listen inside for the expression without a tongue, they may hear His voice of love. For many it seems to be a mystery that is beyond them but that is only because it is hard to give up and be trusting that He will speak His speech of love. All knew this WORD when we were little.

This is how it was with my teachers. I respected them and listened to their word but I also could not ignore the WORD from the Teacher within. I was learning their words of the mind but not the heart. They taught me from their great Book of Truth and that I too believe it is. But, they read the Book with the mind only without balancing their understanding with Spirit's WORD from the heart. I had many contradictions set up inside me and it was hard to hear the Eternal One.

A loving Creator does not divide up His children. He does not leave some out in the cold wind and call only a few into the warm cabin. He cannot abandon His creation because He would be forsaking Himself for He is all in all. I could see if people thought that the Creator was dividing up the world then it was acceptable for them to do the same. This is why there is much division and hatred among people. They have wrong understanding of the way the Creator, Father of all, views His children. Many think there is partiality shown by Creator.

This was a turned around understanding of His unconditional love and oneness. I talked of these things with my teachers. They said I was only having wishful thinking and I did not understand the way of God. But, if this was His way then He was not an all-powerful God or an all-knowing God or an all-loving God. If He was loving and all-powerful and all-knowing then He would make sure of a way to bring His children out of the cold wind to be with Him forever. But, because it was said some were left out in the cold then He was not loving or all-knowing or all-powerful. This was not the Great Teacher that was living in my heart. I was sad for their misunderstanding of what the Eternal One was really like. They were not balancing their mind and heart. I knew that someday they would again see Him as He really was. Maybe it would not be clearly perceived again until they passed from this life. But, just as all people will hear it again when they are drawn into His warm cabin, so too my teachers would again surely hear the WORD from eternity that is not spoken with a worldly tongue.

More and more I was saddened and I knew Spirit was sad too. I asked Spirit what I should do and in the spring during Iskigamizige giizis (Maple Sugar Moon) I understood. I was walking outside and heard Wewe (geese) flying overhead. They were going back to the north. I looked to see them and hear their voices because I missed them in my life. As I was standing there two downy feathers from them floated into my hand and the Voice within said clearly that I too was to follow the Wewe north and take the downy feathers. I knew what this meant. In a few weeks the school year was done and after that return trip north I stayed home. I know that I disappointed my elders in the south but it was better to listen and obey one's heart.

I soon found Adik again and her long hair and big soft eyes like the Caribou drew me to marry her. This was good for me and her too.

I have much more to say about the truth that all is covered by the Love and that all people are one and we are one with the Creator. But, this is a long letter.

Just as it is for everyone to learn these things for themselves so I had to go through these times to learn. Tulugaq Kagagi, you might go through a time when the Teacher within will be quiet or silenced. Do not be worried because Spirit is always waiting for you to say hello again and be asked to speak a little louder. He never leaves you. He never forsakes you. Nothing can separate you from the Eternal Lover even though He may seem not to be there for a long time. Remember, His connection to you in your beginning was not your decision. He is the one that chose to camp within and He will stay because He likes your campsite. It is the same for all the children of the Creator. He is a good Father and does not leave you even when you find it hard to know He is near. This is for each person to learn.

This was a long letter. My fingers are tired from writing. I will roll this up and put it away for you. I think I will also give you the two downy feathers.

Love,
Mishomis (Grandfather) Minominike Gissis Makwa (Rice Moon Bear)

Letter Five
1—Waatebagaa Giizis 1931
(Leaves Changing Color Moon)

Tulugaq Kagagi —
  Before I say what I have been led to write,
Adik says I must write something about Creator.
Adik wants me to say that the Great Mystery is not
a man or a woman. I often call Great Spirit in
my letters by "He" which is a male but that is just
my way. Creator is not a man nor a woman.
Creator is both and neither. The Eternal One is
Being, but not a human being. But, I use "He." It
is just my way. Adik wanted me to say this and
she is correct that I should, because to
understand God we are helped if we know the
Eternal One has traits of woman and man. But,
still I will say "He" because it is just my way.

  It is not too long of a time before ice will come.
First will be on grass, next on the small rocks and
slowly growing out into the still pond waters. The
poplar trees are yellow and tamarack will soon
be turning too. Zììshììb (Ducks) and wewe
(geese) are taking their journey to the south. You
can see from this that they are smarter than we
are. They know it is easier to live in the direction
where the sun goes this time of year.

  I will tell you a little about the teaching of the
four directions. There is much teaching in the

four directions Creator has given us. Just like in all His handiwork He is telling us about Himself. You can never come to an end of learning wonderful things about Creator. He has given us the great Book of Truth that was written down by another tribe of people on the other side of the world long ago. My Ininiwok (people) did not write things down but passed them on by spoken words. Long before the Ancient of Days revelation in the book, He gave us His creation, which reveals Him to us. By observing Creator's works and listening to your heart, His truth will come to you. So, here are little seeds for you to ponder when looking to the four directions.

The Wabun (East) (Its sacred color is red like blood) is where the sun rises and the Spirit speaks to us of the way His light rises and shines on your path. This way you do not have to walk too long in darkness. I believe your path is a deep traveling and with the light in your heart you will walk far on the journey you choose. Acknowledge Spirit and He will direct your path to be straight. The sunrise of the Wabun (East) is teaching that darkness will not last longer than is okay for you to handle. It only seems long and unending when you are in it. So it is with the darkness that will come at times into everyone's life. The sun rises early in some seasons of the year and later in others. Sometimes the dark seems to last long but the light always comes. This is the promise of Wabun (East). It is the place of new beginnings. Let your trust in His faithfulness keep you during the night when it may be hard. — It is from the Wabun (East) that the moon rises. Moon shows us that His light is burning and will return because the moon is reflecting it. The sun has not gone far. This is a parable that darkness cannot overcome light. — Stars show their faces first in the Wabun (East). Though their lights seem to be little, they are good guides for our journey, telling us our direction if we look to them. So, always look to the light no matter how little it seems — The Wabun (East) is from where the long rains come. The long rains can be dreary but without them things cannot grow. So, do not curse the times of long rain in your life because the Creator is giving you wisdom to grow. Some things in life appear good and some bad but all are used in the perfect shaping of your soul. There is never-ending teaching for you to learn from the direction of the rising sun. The Teacher can show you these things and you can see them in the great Book of Truth if you read it with your heart.

The Zhawan (South) (its sacred color is yellow) is the place from where the warm wind brings back life and wakes up the land to grow again. Our brothers and sisters the birds know this and because they cannot store up food they fly to Zhawan (South). The Spirit is like the south wind. When It blows all things become born anew. They are resurrected from their sleep by the Master of Life. We may not hear the wind coming or know just how it performs this miracle, but the Creator does everything at the proper time. Has there ever been a year when the Zhawan (South) did not send the life giving wind? Never. Is there any place where the south cannot blow its wind? No place. The farther north you go into the cold, the more influence the South wind has. You see, wherever a human being is the wind of His Spirit reaches in His perfect timing and gives life. Some years, spring comes early, some years later. It is not for us to judge if His wind is held back for a time. Zhawan (South) shows us the promise of new life after we fall asleep in this one. It is for all people and all creation. It is a universal happening. — There is much more for you to discover from Zhawan (South).

The Ninggabeun (West) (its sacred color is black) is the place where the sun hides itself and then night comes. The night calls us to look within. It pushes us to rest so that we are not always busy and paying no heed to what is important. It slows us so we will ponder. As the day grows older in the Ninggabeun (West) and coolness of twilight comes we are drawn to seek and walk with the One called Ancient of Days. We do good to listen to this calling so that our sleep is peaceful. — There is much prairie to the

Ninggabeun (West) and tall mountains also are planted there. From high up on mountains it is like you can see the end of all things and from the prairie too because there is no tree to be blocking your observing. The Teacher speaks in this that if we look within to the place where things do not block our view, like on the prairies, and, if we patiently raise our hearts up high, like the mountains, even though it may be a hard climb, we will see beyond the understanding of our limited minds and peace will walk inside us. — Ninggabeun (West) also was home to great herds of mashkode biziki (bison). Most are gone now because of disrespect and greed. We do not have this powerful living creature in this area but from him the people received all they needed to live. The great mashkode biziki (bison) of Ninggabeun is a likeness of the greatness of God. He gives us all the medicine we need to be sustained in this life and the next. The early ones of the West, before they had horses, trusted mashkode biziki (bison) to return from his wanderings and give them what was needed. He always did, and so this, too, shows us Creator's faithfulness. — The great light, the sun, gives life to all things and everyday it is traveling across the sky to the West. It is saying to us that through the western door all life will pass. As darkness falls on us in this life we will follow the Light of Life through that beautiful door. The setting of the sun gives us comfort that as life passes there is beauty that is waiting for us. — There is unlimited speaking in the four directions. Hear them. It is for you to learn your own truth.

The Giwaydin (North) (its sacred color is white) is the place of wisdom and silence. The north is white snow, gray rock and blue sky. — The white snow speaks of the white hair of elders who have lived long and have much knowledge. There is great quiet in the Giwaydin (North), which tells us that to become wise we must be quiet within.   — The dark blue sky of the Giwaydin (North) is filled with clean air and is bright and crisp. This is like the times of clarity when we see our oneness with the Creator. All things become clear, there is no cloud making a shadow and the Spirit is fresh, cool and good in our breath. — The gray rocks are the oldest of all things. They are the Grandfathers of the world. Unlike sand, they are solid, making our world steady and secure. This is a teaching that if we build on the Eternal Rock of the Creator Who does not change or move from His opinions of us we will know that we are secure and steady in His hand. — I have heard and seen drawings that the whale lives in the far Giwaydin (North). He is greatest of all creatures. Yet, the powerful mountain that he is will be nothing unless he rises up to the surface to breath the delicate Breath of Life. No matter how strong we believe we are, we are nothing without the Spirit of Life. —

There are many things of the north that speak to us. Consider the powerful white bear, the great hidden sea filled with life under the ice, the seasons of no darkness or of no light, the flocks of birds so many there is no number for them. You will be shown truths that are from the beginning of all things when you seek to listen to His speaking through Giwaydin.

We have traveled the great circle of the world with the four directions. The little I have mentioned which is speaking in the creation about our Maker is only one small droplet of understanding out of all the clouds of the world. There is never-ending teaching coming from His creation. It is there for each person to learn in their own time when they are open and the Teacher within and without sees fit.

Many read only His Book of Truth that is printed and know nothing of the Book of Truth written in His creation long before man even put marks on paper. These who only read the printed Word can easily misunderstand. His Creation is His Word as well. The Creator has given us both for a reason and there is no contradiction between them. They are in harmony.

When I was writing in this letter about the direction Ninggabeun (West) I heard some snorting off beyond the alder bushes and blackberries like maybe a moose or caribou. Adik says that James, Peepeelee and you, are still in need of a little meat for the winter so I will see if it is a small one and if it is willing to give itself away. There is no need to be greedy for a big fellow or to worry about having enough. God knows what is needed.

Grandmother Adik says to tell you to eat more because you need to gain weight. You are too skinny for white boy and need to put on fat for winter like our people are smart to do. Eat more pemmican. Drink canned milk from Brochet store and you will make her happy.

Until I see you next time.

Love,
Mishomis (Grandfather) Minominike Gissis Makwa (Rice Moon Bear)

Letter Six
2 —Waatebagaa Giizis 1931
(Leaves Changing Color Moon)

Tulugaq Kagagi —
It is getting cooler and leaves on trees are changing. The animals are getting their full fur and hair for winter that is coming.

In the last letter when I talk about Wabun (east) and Ninggabeun (west) I write a lot about light and darkness. I had a bawazigaywin (dream) while I was taking a nap today. Today is very warm for this time of the year, Waatebagaa giizis. I fell asleep with my head under my upside down canoe. I lay there to keep the sun out of my eyes. Because of this bawazigaywin (dream), it is my understanding I am to write again a little more. When time comes for you to read and understand maybe it is that you will need this extra teaching. Maybe the Spirit is telling me that you will spend much time in darkness and wonder if there really is light in the life of man or if the light was only in your path when you were young. Many people loose heart wondering if joy and excitement of life was only for when they were not yet grown. It is easy to be lost in the concerns of our life. We can get ill in our hearts. So now I will tell you my dream ....

I dreamt I was a little boy in my father and mother's cabin. She was sewing up a hole in my shirt right over where my heart would be. The hole was almost stitched up when she looked down at me saying she was not going to finish it. She was going to leave a little opening so that light could always get in. After I put my shirt back on I wonder about this in my dream. Then my mother was gone and I was alone. The window and the door of our cabin were letting in the sun and I saw her thimble on the table. I lifted up the thimble and it came to my mind in the dream that the darkness under the thimble did not go out into the room and make things darker. This made me feel good. Then I saw an overturned rice basket in the corner. I went to it and turned it over. The darkness was bigger under it than under the thimble. Still the room did not get any darker when the blackness flowed out from under the rice basket. Over by the door was a big empty wooden barrel. I took off the cover and still the room was filled with light. Even though there was much darkness inside the barrel it could not dim the sunlight in the room. I was amazed that the darkness could not overcome the light. Then in my dream I pushed a chair over to the barrel. I crawled up inside and pulled the cover over my head. It was very dark with no light, even after my eyes adjusted and got bigger. I was sad and afraid and I tried to lift off the cover, but it was too heavy and stuck. I was in the barrel for long time and I was growing bigger like I was aging. The darkness and breathing was oppressive. Finally I think I could hear someone working on the barrel cover and I faintly hear the voice of my father. He lifted the cover just a little and a bright tiny stream of light peeked in. It shines into the hole left in my shirt by my mother and I am filled with happiness. After I was free from the barrel, it was very strange because the bright tiny stream of light was now shinning outward from the hole in my shirt and making the world brighter…

This was my dream as I napped under the canoe. I am confident it is for you to read and think about. Wherever our lives have taken us, we gain much through our unique experiences. We can shine back to others from dark times in our lives and from good times. When we are in hard and dark times our Father knows. He will not let the heavy cover be stuck closed forever. The light and air will come to us. Listen to this dream. It is a teaching. Listen to your dreams. They may be a revealing thing. This is each person to learn.

Love,
Mishomis Minominike Gissis Makwa
(Grandfather)

Chapter Five: Years of Distraction

After reading through more letters the previous evening I awoke with the dawn only a few hours later. A beam of light spilled across my eyes through a crack in the chinking of the cabin. The raspy laugh between Ravens on the porch roof reminded me of my name from years ago. Grandfather's words were speaking in my heart and I felt that the patterns of judgment in my mind were being exposed for the delusions and bias they were. It was uncomfortable, but good. A voice within, something I heard more effortlessly when I was young, seemed to again be whispering. The voice of the Teacher? Recollections of a long forgotten and beloved friend made me smile. Sitting up on the edge of my small bed, I lowered my head in meekness, wondering how I had been so preoccupied as to ignore this Voice within for so long.

Nearly a generation had passed since I first left for school in the south and pursued a career. Many voices had begun to fill my mind as I grew up. Now it seemed they had been a subtle and nearly thorough distraction. Busyness, the uncertainties and disappointments of life, fantasies of possessions, my profession, even my education to understand this inner Voice seemed to have contributed to the clamor overriding His whispers. My heart had not gone deaf. My Friend and Teacher had never left, but was only patiently waiting for me to listen.

The letters were the catalyst that again opened my inner ear to the Beloved voice. I may have been distracted and wandered off, but He stood on the porch watching with open arms. I may have lost thought of Him or as may be the case with some, never acknowledged, experienced or been aware of His presence. The truth, however, is clear. He is always there. As Minominike had taught and the call of this morning's raven was reminding me—Raven is never alone. Tulugaq Kagagi would never again forget.

Letters Seven through Ten

Waatebagaa Giizis

Letter Seven
3 —Waatebagaa Giizis 1931
(Leaves Changing Color Moon)

Tulugaq Kagagi —
This is my third letter during this moon. Adik is thinking that maybe I am turning into the white English writer she called Longspear. I told her the man's name was William Shakespeare and then she laughs.

She says — William Shakespeare must have been a useless hunter. What good is a spear if all you do is shake it? If, when Peepeelee was young in the far north and her father would go after seals through the ice by just shaking his spear, the only way the seals would be giving themselves away is if they laughed themselves to death. Maybe that is a secret hunting method that only this Shakespeare knows. He has a silly name.

Adik brings many smiles to my face when she makes jokes. I will have to ask Peepeelee if her father just shakes his spear at the seals like the Englishman.

You are now over three winters old and will be turning to four in a couple moons. There is a Kagagi (raven) who likes to remind me every winter around your birthday to make you a toy. On your first birthday I carved you two little

Kagagis. One named Tulugaq and other Kagagi. This was for your namesake. I made them big enough so you could not swallow them because you put everything in your mouth. Once you swallowed a tiny stone from the lakeshore but it came out okay. Peepeelee worried for a time but with the help of fat from fish and some berries in your food everything come out fine. I made you a fish out of spruce for birthday number two. I made it in two parts and put a joint in it with wire loops so that it moves like Kinoje (pike). For third birthday I made you three spruce dogs after the dogs at your cabin. I wrote their names on them — Kaniq, Nanuk, and Dende. Peepeelee give names Kaniq (Frost) and Nanuk (Bear) to the old ones. These names are from her language. James called the young dog Dende (Bullfrog) from our tongue. I'm going to start making you a canoe to float in the lake for your fourth birthday. I will carve it big enough for the Kagagis (ravens), the Kinoje (pike) and your three little spruce dogs to ride in. Maybe you will have these toys even when you grow up. If not, this letter will remind you about them.

So, I have a short teaching for this letter that is like your toys I created. I carved them all from spruce but each is different. Here is the story.

The people of the world are like the stones on the lakeshore near your cabin. Everyone has been made different and is a gift to the world. Each has been given special qualities by the action of the Creator. Each is different and has a unique place on the shore of His world. Yet each is equal.

Let me tell you how this equality is true. I will show you something about every stone on our shoreline. Every stone has the same source. They have all come from the one great Rock. This Rock is the foundation that earth itself is built on. It comes from the deep unseen place in the earth. No stone on our shore can exist without this Rock. It rises up from the earth and makes every one of the stones as it gives itself away. In this way all the stones are unique but all are of One.

So it is the people of the earth. We are all from the One source, but unique. We are different shape or color, like the stones. We reflect the sun differently. We have different outlook on the world. Some people, like stones, seem hard, some rough or smooth, some break easy. Yet all have come from the One source. Each shows us of the One Rock because they are all brothers and sisters from the One Rock.

This is like the toys I carved for you. They are different but they have come from One source, the spruce tree and they are all the work of One set of hands. My hands. They have gifts that are different but still they are related, equal and same because of their source and maker.

Sometimes people say that God is not the Father of all because of differences they see, like people doing things differently and thinking differently, or because some people do not have understanding of God the same. Because of this they divide themselves from one another and start to fear each other and this may grow into hate for each other. This is foolishness! Can you imagine the stones on the shore of Reindeer lake thinking because some are white and some gray or some are round and others long that they do not have the same Source? I haven't heard of any stones believing such nonsense and hating one another. Our oneness in His family is not because we do things all the same or all think the same or are all round instead of long. We are one because we have one Source, One Creator, One Father. Nothing can break apart this family. Just as the stones eventually return to become part of the great Rock of the earth, so too all people will be reunited in our one Source and Father of all. It is very sad that so few listen to the Teacher within telling them this truth that creation speaks to us. If people could hear this truth, much pain would fly from the world and great joy over our unity in the Rock would sing out.

This is main reason why my heart and mind were in conflict when I was at seminary. It was thought that a person was not in His one big family until that person asked to be in it. But, if this was so, from what Father did anyone come in the first place? It was assumed at the seminary that there was not the one family of God. In this way they broke up the unity of His world. They divided what the Great Spirit had joined together by His love for all people. They would not consider that maybe everyone already was in the one family of God and that they just needed to be told of this oneness with the Creator, if they didn't know of it. Many people are not whole because they do not know of their Oneness in the Spirit. By telling them what already is a reality they can believe it and peace can come to their minds.

So, you see that just like your toys have all been made of one tree by one set of hands, and all the stones on the shoreline of our big lake are from one source, so too it is with the people of the whole world. We are all His, whether we know it or believe it.

Isn't that a good and strong truth? In the knowing of this there is a medicine to drive away much suffering.

Our old dog, Willie, is standing outside the door whining. We let him sleep in the cabin when the nights get cold. He has a canvas bag to rest on by the stove. I will let that spoiled dog in and stop writing for tonight. Grandmother Adik is snoring in her chair. Sometimes at night the noises of old Willie and Adik make this cabin sound like it is filled with a nasty and dreadful manitou (spirit) that would scare away the biggest makwa (bear).

Good night to you.

Love,
Mishomis Minominike Gissis Makwa

Letter Eight
1—Binaakwii Giizis 1931
(Falling Leaves Moon)

Tulugaq Kagagi —

I have been writing much about the one family to which all people belong and about the one Father of all. It is hard for many to understand this in their minds because they have been taught a different thing. It is this misunderstanding that causes much pain in the world.

When we think that Creator does not see each human equally, then we, too, believe we should not see each equally with same love. It is funny, yet sad, how each person that believes this way thinks that Creator sees just their group as on His side and that only they are children of His. This is a contradictory thing. Each imagines the other is not accepted by the Father. Everyone has different reasons for this. There are so many invented reasons that it must be there is no one that is accepted because each group will have a reason that the other group is wrong until everybody is falling under some reason and they are cast away. People are very convinced that they are right and that they must make others think and do as they do to please their God. But, since there can only be the one Creator how can He be against Himself?

From the heart of each person is a long string that connects us to all our brothers and sisters. It is the string of love coming from the Love that is God. If you think on this string of love with your heart you can see all people as the Great Lover sees them and holds them and ties them to Himself with the string. The more you let His love be in you and know the reality that He is your never-ending Lover, the more it will transform you and flow out from you and soften those in the world who have misunderstood. You will be like a light on a moonless rainy night for those who are out on the big Reindeer Lake looking for direction. It is the Great Lover who changes us from inside out. It is the Great Lover who loves through us.

Zahgidiwin (Love) is what the Creator is. Zahgidiwin (Love) is what the Spirit is. Zahgidiwin (Love) is His whole expression and is demonstrated in all His creation and in the form of a Man too. Love is the beginning and end of all things. Love is the great giveaway I have mentioned in my letters. Love cannot help but give itself away. Because Creator is love He gives Himself away to make all things and give life. The Great Lover has emptied Himself for the creation and still does so. This love is forgiving and asks for nothing back. (Do you see my play on words? 'For-giving'?) He holds us to no debt but pardons our weak ability to do this life right. He empties Himself out in mercy to be with us in our weakness. This is what Zahgidiwin (Love) does—gives itself away.

The One Rock of the foundation of the earth gives away to have expression in the stones. The stones give away to the plant so they have life. The plants give away to moose and caribou and beaver so they live. Moose and caribou and beaver give away to wolf and to me so we can live. I must learn to give myself away also so that others can find life from me. It is Love that causes all things to be. This is greatest teaching. The Great Love gives itself away so that all have life. When you taste this Love you, too, cannot help but give yourself away. This Love is the beginning and end of all things. When this Love is allowed to be big in us we have no fear to be giving ourselves away. We have no fear to do this. We can lose ourselves and in that we find our real life, who we are and our oneness with all people, all of creation, all of the universe. We find that we are one with the Great One and always have been. We see that the universe is not a fearful and angry place but is ultimately caring for us.

So, when it comes that you hear of much pain in the world or experience it from another or maybe you even give pain to another, it is mostly because we humans do not know or hold tightly to the string and the Spirit of Love. We believe in the illusion of being separated from each other. We believe in the illusion of being separated from oneness with Him. We are afraid because of insecurity of thinking we are alone and must hold on hard to life in this hostile universe. But, this is a lie. The universe is loving because the Creator is loving. This love of the One Great Lover is heard in the voice of the Teacher within.

The journey of all people is made more wonderful when they walk holding the hand of their Lover. Just like when you and I go walking. We hold hands and you can walk a little easier. Even when the walking is rough if we hold hands you won't fall as hard and my hand can help you. Sometimes I even carry you through the heavy brush and big stones. You will probably not remember, but I never just go and pick you up. I always let you struggle with the brush or big stones until you reach to me. This way I respect you. Creator is like this, too.

This is for each to learn.

Zahgidiwin (Love),
Mishomis   Minominike   Gissis   Makwa
(Grandfather Rice Moon Bear)

Letter Nine
2—Binaakwii Giizis 1931
(Falling Leaves Moon)

Tulugaq Kagagi —
Here is a picture for you. This is Binaakwii giizis, moon of falling leaves. Creator caused them to be and now He calls them from their place on each tree. They have given shade and protection to birds in rough weather and made their tree proud of having them. They were one color when little buds, then grew and turned to green, now they are yellow and some brown or orange or red. They have gone through life and it made each one unique. Some fly away easily. Some hang on to their branch longer. Each leaf was separate from the others, but was still one with them through the tree. When they fall it is a pleasant thing to watch them float away carried by the noodinoon (winds). It is like a Spirit wind taking them back to their Maker. He gently sets them all down to lie on the ground at the same level. Teaching in this their equality and oneness. It is like this with all people. We go through life and our uniqueness is revealed. We are even at different levels on the tree and on different branches, but still, at the end, the Spirit takes each one the same and shows us that we are all loved equally and without conditions.

It is a beautiful time of the year.

Love,
Mishomis   Minominike

Letter Ten
  3—Binaakwii Giizis 1931
  (Falling Leaves Moon)

Tulugaq Kagagi —
The young moose was near the cabin again some days ago. I am very thankful to him. He knows that we were short on meat for the winter and so came to give himself away. He had a short life. Maybe two snows or three but it was complete. His spirit is gone back to God who gave it. Maybe he is browsing again in the next life. Adik and I thanked him and I am sure he said we are welcome to use his body.

I have been writing much of the oneness and unity that is all the universe because of Creator's love. I will always write much of this because it is the final truth. When we learn it we can be at peace with ourselves and life. Only then do we become truly alive. This is the special thing that man has been given. We are gifted a journey of discovery. It can be a hard path, but that is okay. When you taste of Creator's goodness in this life or meet Him when you pass through the western door, you will not question the journey. You will be at peace with it and know it was a unique path for making you a unique soul in all the universe. I know that you will see this before the western door is opened for you.

Our animal relations know what they are from birth and walk their path without question. Namegossika (Trout) will do what the Creator has gifted Namegossika to do. Osprey will do what is put inside from her beginning. Jangweshe (Mink) will follow the path of his spirit without having to think it out. Namegossika (Trout), Osprey, Jangweshe (Mink), all our animal relations do not open their gift. It is already opened for them. By listening and watching them we can learn much—but that is for another letter. The young moose, too, was doing what was his gift until he was called upon to give himself away.

We people are different. We have been given a gift that is not opened for us. It is our honor, our privilege to open it and find our uniqueness. Each of us is unique like the stones on Reindeer's shore. But, unlike the stones who patiently let the work of the Creator form them, we people often resist His shaping. We don't know that He is helping to open up the gift put inside us. We fight against Him when we should not struggle. We close the eyes and ears of our heart and so are not guided in the way He wishes to take us. We resist much what we should not and so cannot receive teaching within our situations. We think we are better at knowing the gift than He is. When we do this, we do not listen to the Teacher within, then the beautiful gift is harder to be opened for us. Unlike our animal relations it is our privilege to find the specialness of who we are and embrace it and live it out. I am still learning much on my journey.

A few days ago, it was very sunny and warm, even though it is Binaakwii giizis (Falling Leaves Moon). I was over to visit you, James and Peepeelee, to tell of the generosity of the young moose and bring some meat. There are no mosquitoes or flies out because of the frosts, so you were playing on the shore without any clothes. This was a picture of your place on the journey. You are innocent and free. You are knowing nothing of being ashamed because you are living in the voice of the Teacher who tells you of the benevolence of all things. There is nothing to fear and you accept life as full of joy and have no concern of tomorrow. Even when there is pain, it is received and experienced and you go back to playing on the shores of the Lord. Being with no clothes is as it should be. There is no reason to cover up our Beings. There is no feeling of shame or of fears. Life is beautiful and full of wonder.

But, this is not where we stay as we grow. Other voices come in and we begin to listen to them. Slowly we begin to live in them and hear less of the Great Father's voice telling us all is okay. It becomes harder to take off our clothes and play. We do not trust the love of our Father inside our heart or in the creation. We start to make everything complex. Life loses innocence and maybe pains and fears make us close up like a clam. We think it is necessary to protect our self. We grow insecure. The heart gets caught like in one of my traps that clamps onto the leg of a mink or like a snare that catches the waabooz (rabbit). For some, who have a cruel childhood or are taught wrong or have a hard grief, the trap and snare hold them very tight. For some, they can recall the freedom and acceptance, but it is still complicated to be naked again and to be carefree in this loving universe. This is where most people live the big part of their lives. They are not aware of the goodness of the Creator and so they must have control over their world to feel secure. Many also look for happiness by getting many possessions. These things eat up their life and cause forgetfulness of where the deeper joy is found by resting in the arms of our Maker. It is very much this way in the south country. You will know this in life. It is for all people to travel this path of more or less resisting and not listening. It is the privilege of all people to experience this journey but hopefully without resisting. Our animal relations do not have the honor of a path of learning. The gift of their journey is already opened for them on their walk, as I said.

Our journey never stops. As we walk our life path we are to come to be enlightened that control and possessions and fear and insecurity are an illusion that keep you from seeing Creator's real life and freedom in His universe. (Remember the story of how the first man and woman in the world were deceived into thinking there were things to be feared and how Raven returned the Light of the World?) By grace of the Creator we are to taste again the joy of playing naked and not be afraid. As we are drawn by Him to listen again, the trap and snare should begin unfastening and let our heart to fly away. This freedom of life can seem to be a hard thing to find again but it is right there as our inheritance. It is freely for us to live in again and rediscover. It is always right in front of us but sometimes it is hard to see like the tracks of a small bird in the sand. It has never been taken away, but being a human means it is allowed to be hidden so we can know the wonder of its beautiful joy. When we see it again we will know that playing naked is what we were created to do.

So, we discover by our path there is a deep love and thankfulness that we take hold of. We alone can then say thank you from our spirit to Him. This is a special thing for us as people that the Creator Father has allowed. He has not given this journey to our animal relations. As it was for me, so it is for you and for each person to learn and not be trapped in the illusion of control and fear and shame. Our journey is a circle like the great circle of the earth. We are born innocent, but we grow up to be thinking we have to be protecting and defending our life. However, we are to grow beyond this and rediscover that to be really alive is to abandon ourselves to the grace of not caring to save ourselves. We are then freed again to learn to play without clothes as it should be. Only here do we find the wonder of real life in letting ourselves be at the mercy of our Loving Creator. Sadly, many do not taste much of this life on their journey.

It has been given to me that you will not stay in this place of being afraid of nakedness. After you have walked long you will taste again His freedom. On your journey you will begin to slowly learn to live in holy carelessness until you come to your last giveaway and pass through the western door.

I have read this letter to Adik. She wants me to write for her again.

- — -

Hello little naked boy. I heard about you playing in the sun by the lake. It is so right to know we are loved by all around us and we do not have to be afraid or ashamed. I still take my bath in the river like that when it is warm. Grandfather does too. In a few days I will be bringing some more of the young moose over to Peepeelee. We will have a big feast with moose, berries and fish and beans from the store at Brochet. I'm sure James and Grandfather will make plenty of noise with the beans. I love you almost as much as our Creator loves you. — Grandmother Adik

     - — -

   Adik doesn't know this but I'm adding into this letter that she makes the noise with the beans too! Not just me and James. So you can laugh about this someday when you read it.

   Love,
   Mishomis Minominike Gissis Makwa

Chapter Six: Spirit/Freedom

Sitting at our cabin table reading Minominike's letters with the image of my young, free and naked body playing on the shore of the lake, I became acutely aware of my present enslavement to the protection and advancement of my life. Regardless of one's degree of external freedom, it appears it is overwhelmingly true that nearly all people are enslaved to themselves. To be caught up in the preservation of our lives is to be in bondage. I had allowed my true being to be detoured into the prison of self.

I put down Minominike's tenth letter to consider the metaphor of the season in which it was written. Binaakwii Giizis, Falling Leaves Moon, is cautioning of the cold to come. It is a time when the preservation of life appears foremost in the activities of the world yet not a time designed for permanence. Preparing and planning for the future is a natural part of life, but I had allowed the prudence of foresight to mutate and dominate. I began to see that I had become self-protective, fearful, and had lost my ability to play naked on the shore.

Walking out of the cabin and down to the lake, I looked backward in time and caught glimpses of myself clothed only in the presence and freedom of life. At one time, I had played in holy carelessness, naturally and joyfully experiencing existence. That freedom was not gone. It was only suppressed by self-protection and fear. A fear that was beginning to dissolve as the fire of the truth of who I really was began to be rekindled by the letters of Minominike.

"The person who tries to preserve his life will lose it," Jesus had said. It is in knowing that we are ultimately held and preserved in the loving arms of our Creator Father, that the freedom to live openly, nakedly, honestly and vulnerably is experienced. This is the intended path of life, losing it in the arms of God in order to wholly find it.

The expression of my understanding could be confirmed no other way. Once again, naked, I stood on the stones of the shore of Reindeer before my Creator. I had become the metaphor of freedom, the wind of the Spirit having full view of my being. "Come play with me," I imagined Him saying as the cold dark water baptized me again in newness of life.

Letters Eleven through Thirteen

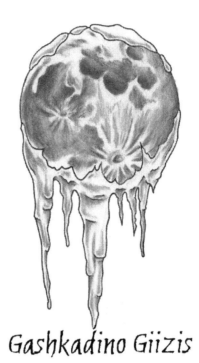

Gashkadino Giizis

Letter Eleven
1—Gashkadino Giizis 1931
(Ice Is Forming Moon)

Tulugaq Kagagi —
I heard it was very exciting at your cabin the
other night. You might remember this when you
grow up, but maybe not, so I will write it.

It was before the sun came up when James
heard your dogs growling. They were tied up for
the night in front of your cabin. They started in
with a mad barking. Your father lit a lantern
and yelled at them from the door. When he did
that he heard a "woof" and a bench fell over
alongside the door. He had the door open just a
little and something slammed it in his face and
almost knocked the lantern out of his hands. The
door flew back open and there was a black
makwa looking right at him. James shouted out
of being afraid and the big black boar makwa
took off right into the door again and slammed
it shut again. The dogs were on one side of him
and the cabin on the other. This time James
could hear the big fellow scrambling to get his
bearings and he ran off toward the dogs. He was
going so fast the dogs couldn't even get a bite out
of his hinder. With all this noise Peepeelee woke
up and you did, too. The yelling scared you and
you were crying for some time, James said. Your
father thinks makwa was looking for a place to

spend the winter under your cabin. Peepeelee found where nanuk (bear), this is what Peepeelee calls him in her tongue, had been digging a little under where your room was added on to the cabin. What do you think of that?

I had to take Adik into Brochet to see about pains she was having in her arm. She was feeling ill, too, for some days after the pains. The visiting mission doctor called it a small attack of her odayin (heart). He is a kind man who looks after you, too. She stayed in town for a couple days and also for almost two weeks at your house resting in your bed. She is doing better now. She is not to do heavy work so I will do more and you and James will help, too. You are a big help even though you are not yet past four snows old.

That is all for this letter. I wanted to tell you of the big black boar makwa and of Adik. I will write soon about the things that are signs of a heart that God is shaping to reflect Him. Adik's heart has spoken to me to write about this.

Love,
Mishomis Minominike Gissis Makwa

Letter Twelve
2—Gashkadino Giizis 1931
(Ice Is Forming Moon)

Tulugaq Kagagi —
Adik is doing well. She is happy to be home. She has a smile about all things and especially about you. Now, I will write what she says.

.—.—.

You need to come over soon and stay for a while. I wish to hold you next to my heart to give it strength. That would be a good thing. We can play hide the thimble and listen to Grandfather tell stories by the warm stove. I have a big new colorful blanket that I got from the store when I was in Brochet because of my sickness. Bring your stuffed mink along to sleep with and some other toys.

Love,   Nokomis (Grandmother) Adik
.—.—.

So, here are the teachings that show you that the Great Spirit is shaping you like He wishes a son and daughter to be. I told you in last letter that I would write them to you because the situation with Adik's heart inspired me to do so.

First teaching:

This is the teaching of Maiingan (wolf). He shows us that humility is a place in which God reigns in our hearts. Humility is a sign that even though you may be strong and able to promote yourself like Maiingan, you do not take the opportunity to do so. This is the way God is. He does not puff Himself up and force His way. Even though the One Who made us has every right to do so, Creator gives us room to be and does not push us to the side. He stoops down and serves us His good things even though He is the Greater One. He is happy to be with us even when we ignore Him and do not acknowledge His presence. This is truly humility and when we have a heart that is humble, like Maiingan, we can know the Creator is having joy over us. So happy are you when you are humble.

Second teaching:

This is the teaching that Makwa (bear) shows us. He has much courage but it is not courage in his own power. It is the courage of faith in the power of Another. He goes about his life from spring to fall and fills himself with what Creator gives. He does not store up a cache of food, but takes what is freely given. When it turns cold he does not worry but trusts His Maker to see him through the long sleep to spring. We, too, can have this courage of faith in times when it is cold in our lives. The Teacher within will tell you that you do not need to fear the cold. Your heart can rest in knowing that what you need, the Owner of All Things will freely give you. If you are in a hard place, He can give you a peaceful rest. At the end of this life, too, remember the courage and faith of Makwa and it will be well. He goes to sleep with no fear and wakes to new life in the new world of spring. He is a good picture for us to learn from. It shows over and over of the truth of Geezus, Who long ago came back to life after sleeping in death. Listen to your heart and let the courage of faith in His presence with you cause you to grow and have peace. You will be happy.

Third teaching:
This is the teaching of love that Kinew (eagle) reveals. He shows many things, but the greatest He shows us is the beautiful love of God. With little effort Kinew soars high in the sky because he is floating on winds of love in his heart. The love will never let Kinew fall, but takes him higher until he cannot be seen. He is taken so high on Creator's love that he calls out. We can hear him calling from the heavens even though he is beyond our sight. He is calling us to come up closer to God with him and ride the winds of this love. He calls us to look within to the great heights of this love already residing in our hearts. There are three loves — the love of the body, the love of a friend and the unconditional love of our Father God. Kinew is telling us that

God's love is absolute and depends on nothing. It is never withdrawn. We can never be separated from it in life or death or the highest or lowest place. In light or darkness it is there. It does not depend on us. Kinew rides on this love high into the sky not even working his wings. It is for him and us to be enjoyed without cost. He lets it take him by resting on the love wind of the Spirit. There is no greater happiness than to have let your heart taste His love. When you find this way you can be at rest and love yourself just as the Creator has made you.

Fourth teaching:

This teaching is from Gichi Sabe (great man of the forest). Some people call him Sasquatch. Tulugaq Kagagi, listen closely to this teaching. Gichi Sabe instructs us about honesty. About being sincere and open with life. Few have ever seen Gichi Sabe because in order to do so you must be as honest and open and sincere as he is. He does not hide himself, but very few will ever get a peek of him unless you become as transparent as he is with your own life. He is a paradox in his teaching, isn't he? You must seek to be seeable if you are to seek to see him. Seeking to be honest and open is a difficult thing because we so easily think me must hide and protect ourselves. The more we hide, the less it is possible to see this one some call Sasquatch. Some do not believe he is real because they do not understand his way. You can believe this or not, but I will describe glimpses I have seen of him in my life. He may look a little different to you if you become honest and transparent enough to see him. This is how he was to me. He puts on no clothing because he is covered with beautiful flowing hair. So he taught me that he hides nothing and is open and honest by this, in not covering himself. He has soft eyes and they looked right into mine. So he taught me that he was letting me look into his heart because he had nothing to hide. We, too, should have nothing to hide. He is much taller than me and his feet were larger than mine, and I have big feet. But, when he walked toward me his steps were not hostile and did not scare me even though he was Gichi Sabe. So he taught me that being honest and open will take fear out of other people when you are in their presence. If in your heart you let honesty steer you to being open, transparent, sincere and real with others and the Creator, it will cause happiness to be in your heart. This is because to be this way with our Creator is to be honest about our need to know His close walk with us. So, be like Gichi Sabe.

I have written enough for tonight. The rest of the teachings will be for next letter. Adik is getting ready for bed and wants me to put out the kerosene light. She says she is cold, too, and wants me to warm up the bed. This is something we have always done during the time when the far north moves down to our Reindeer Lake. I warm up the bed for her and then roll over to my side. You may remember this when you grow up. Maybe not. But, when you sleep at our cabin you sleep between us to keep warm. You do this with Peepeelee and James, too, at this time of the year. Some day you will be wanting to always sleep by yourself, but until that time, it is good to have you. Oh, oh. Adik is sleeping in the chair and snoring again. I must go. Good night.

Love,
Mishomis   Minominike   Gissis   Makwa
(Grandfather Rice Moon Bear)

Letter Thirteen
3 —Gashkadino Giizis 1931
(Ice Is Forming Moon)

Tulugaq Kagagi —
You are visiting our cabin a couple days. You are wrapped up in Adik's new blanket and sleeping with our dog near the wood stove. Adik is making our supper. We are going to have fry bread made with some dried berries and some Kinoje (pike), too. There is a little left over Wewe (Goose) too. After we eat I will finish the teachings I started in last letter.

- — - -

Ah, that was good. We finished up the Kinoje and the Wewe, too. Even the berries are gone. Everything is cleaned and put away. You and Adik are playing a game and Willie, our old dog, is dreaming by the stove. He makes odd noises when he dreams and his feet twitch.

Now I will write more of the teachings I started last letter. Counting the first four there are a total of seven of them that I want to talk of.

This is the **Fifth teaching:**
Ahmek (beaver) shows us about wisdom. Ahmek gives much effort to the work of securing his dam and pond and lodge and food cache. He is always a busy fellow at this. He has set his task

to the things that give him life. It is easy for us people to work at so much that does not give life. Much time is spent going after things we don't need, like more money than is needed, too big of house, lots of dishes or more traps and guns than is needed and this eats up our time and demands attention away from the things that give us life. These things are relationship with family and people in our world and with the Spirit, Who is our peace giver, teacher, and who loves us completely with a love that brings satisfaction to our inner person no matter our situation. When we have this satisfaction and contentment we don't need to chase after so many things. Spirit is life itself and to the Spirit Ahmek wisely keeps his life focused. Ahmek also shows us a hard thing. He usually works and builds in the dark of night. This is a picture to give us hope because in our lives many hard times of physical and mental suffering can come. We may feel like we are surrounded and laboring in the darkness of a never-ending night. But, it is in the night and the dark times of life that great things are being built and taught. After the night passes, we see that Ahmek has built up much wisdom through our experience in the darkness. He has more perfectly built up his dam and lodge and stored more good food during the night. It is so with our lives. The shaping of wisdom in our hearts is often done during the night. So, as hard and fearful as dark times can be, remember the teaching of Ahmek. The day will shine again and you will have been made more perfect. The Master builder knows how to work, especially in the dark.

Sixth Teaching:

Respect, is the teaching of Mashkode Biziki (Bison). Mashkode Biziki lives on the grass lands to the southwest of Reindeer region. I did hear once that there were some Mashkode Biziki over around the Athabasca Lake, too. He is very powerful and large. There are few that would defy him. One might think he is the Lord of the land. But, when you watch him you will notice that as great as he is, he will most of his day be in a posture of honor to the Giver of Life. He will have his great head lowered to the ground in respect to the Greater One. In this way he acknowledges that he is not Lord of the Earth or his life and he is respectful of the One Who is. We do well to consider this when we think we are the shaper and controller of our destiny. Mashkode Biziki (Bison) also does a unique thing. Sometimes the One Lord of the Earth will send storms. When a strong cold wind blows in winter, all creatures turn their backs to the wind. But, Mashkode Biziki does not turn his back. Instead he will face the wind and give it honor and respect even though it is a hard thing. Through the harshest storm he will respect what is being brought his way and not turn his back to avoid it. He receives whatever mysterious gift it may bring. He knows the storms of life will pass and they can leave behind even good. This is hard for us people. Still, there is much to be learned by acknowledging the storms that come in life and facing them head on. So, face head on what may challenge you and respect it for what it may bring.

Seventh teaching:

Mikinaak (Turtle) gives us the teaching of Truth. Living the truth is living these "seven teachings" and trusting in the always present Spirit of Wisdom and Understanding. To live in truth is also to live close to our Mother the Earth just like Mikinaak lives so close. Even when Mikinaak is standing tall on legs he is never more than a small stone above Mother Earth and in the winter he is inside the earth itself. If we have no close ties to Mother Earth, we begin to lack understanding of our dependency on her. We then become thoughtless and uncaring in how she is treated. This is not wisdom. To live in truth by being close to our Mother is to live in thankfulness because she gives us everything we need for our physical bodies. Mikinaak is always laying himself on the breast of our Mother. He cannot rise very far from her. Also, Mikinaak shows us that only by having patience and being quiet do we come to know truth. He is not hurried and he lives a long time. In long life we can come to more understanding of the purpose we are existing for. I have heard that Mikinaak lives longer than all our animal relations. I think this is true because he is patient and quiet and listens to the Spirit lead him. Being patient and quiet inside ourselves lets us walk in truth instead of rushing around in false ways without thinking. This gets us stressed up. You will also see that as people get older they are not in such a hurry and they have more patience like Mikinaak to find out the truth of things. So, think on Mikinaak, be contented and live the truth of these teachings by listening to Him who speaks within.

I have told you only some things that are brought to us by Maiingan (Wolf), Makwa (Bear), Kinew (Eagle), Gichi Sabe (Sasquatch), Ahmek (Beaver), Mashkode Biziki (Bison) and Mikinaak (Turtle). There are never-ending teachings that you can hear from the Father by watching these relations live out the way of the spirit that has been given to them. The "seven teachings" are the building blocks around which we build our lives. The "seven teachings" are always revolving around and coming from the Spirit of God. These things are for each person to discover for themselves. Each is to experience how much the Father of All is dancing over us in joy. In this way we are all unique.

I had to stop several times in writing of this letter. That old dog, Willie, must have had some nightmares again. As I said at the start of the letter, he was whining and his feet were wiggling so much that all of us were laughing at him. You felt bad for him and woke him up twice, but he went right back to his sleeping and dreaming. Maybe he was being scolded by the Creator for chewing his leather harness. He did that bad thing this morning and I scolded him, too. I should have given him a piece of moose hide to chew on so he wouldn't go after the harness I left out. It was partly my fault. I'm thinking the old fellow will be passing on like me and Adik by the time you read this letter. But, you may remember him. I think he is 13 winters old now.

Love,
Mishomis   Minominike   Gissis   Makwa
(Grandfather Rice Moon Bear)

Chapter Seven: Earth Speaks

It was nearing noon and my stomach began to complain. I hadn't carried much food along to the cabin so I put on my jacket and started for Brochet to visit the store. Only a few meters down the path I stopped. I turned and walked back to the place where the old black makwa tried to dig under my little room. He was looking for a place to winter sleep and the depression he chose was still there. James had never filled it in. Wondering what ever became of this night visitor. I imagined his spirit laughing still as he recalled the terror both he and James experienced that night long ago. I smiled, laughed out loud, and headed for the store.

About half way to town an explosion of ravens from the path just ahead startled me. I had rounded a corner without their knowing I was coming. There on the path was the body of a kagagi. I stooped down and discovered she had just died. Her body was still warm and limp in my hands. The dozen or so paying their last respects had scattered to the nearby spruce and birch. They sat silently watching as I gently placed her body on the moss along the side of the path.

A single raven, I supposed to be her mate, flew overhead and perched only several arm lengths away. From inside his chest I could hear low pleading tones. I moved away slowly and watched from a respectful distance. One by one, the congregation returned to the ground until only two ravens sat in the trees. A low murmur of tones and clicks could be heard from the gathering. They seemed to be consoling one another and releasing the spirit of the deceased back to Creator. I took my seat on a rock and wondered at this and the letters I just finished reading.

Maiingan, Makwa, Kinew, Gichi Sabe, Ahmek, Mashkode Biziki, Mikinaak, all the earth people and the earth itself speak to us if we listen. For decades I had been isolated from the original revelation of Creator, boxed in by the walls of steel, glass and concrete, the inorganic and mute. The earth is filled with voices pure and clean. If we have ears to hear we need only listen to the wisdom, joy and beauty surrounding us, bringing us life.

The ravens slowly departed, but I remained. Minominike's short teachings from the earth in these last letters caused me to recall my young winter days going out to lie at night on the ice of Reindeer Lake. Peepeelee would bundle me up in wool and canvas and caution me not to venture too far from shore. Stretched out and looking up at stars and the aurora, closing my eyes and hearing the ice speak as it expanded and shifted, there was never a question that Mother Earth had a voice. Her language was not foreign to my being. She spoke wordless prose of truth from everlasting. My inner being, although so very young, understood these expressions and I would feel myself transported into the timeless.

Letters Fourteen and Fifteen

Manidoo Giizisoons

Letter Fourteen
Manidoo Giizisoons 1931
(Little Spirit Moon)

Tulugaq Kagagi —
This is moon of your birth. Happy birthday to you.

This is also the time of year it is said that the Great Spirit, Gichi Manidoo, the I Am, the Creator, the Ancient of Days took on flesh and became as a man. So it is also said to be the birthday of Wabun Ahnung (Morning Star). The Creator did this to show the world we were wrong in believing He did not love us and that we were deceived in thinking we had to do something to make Him happy over us. This One has many odd names like Counselor, Beginning and End, First Stone, Morning Star, Ageless One, Lamb, Teacher, Rising Sun, The Word. I saw a Lamb once when I was young while in the south at Winnipeg. It had very thick and curly hair. It was a kind and tender animal that followed me around and would not leave me alone. This Lamb was like the Teacher Within, always sticking close by me, always nuzzling me like it wanted to draw my attention and wake me up to show me something.

So, anyway, this taking on the form of a human was foretold through men like Yeshaiah, Daniye'l and Zekar-yah and Johanan in the

Book of Truth. These were of a different tribe on the other side of the earth. The Book said that the Eternal Father of all would do this mysterious thing of being in the body of a man. He would do this to show the world what He was like and that He holds everyone in His embrace. It was also told in the Book, by a man named Yo'el, also from another tribe on the other side of the world that the Great Spirit would live in everyone. Not just some, but everyone. There are many who think His Spirit is only in some but they do not understand with their hearts. I explained this in my earlier letters. It is their way, but they divide up the family of God that He has made as one.

The name given to the One who was the expression of the Great Spirit in flesh was Geezus. He lived with these tribes on the other side of the world. I am sure that you will know all this by time you read these letters. But, I want to tell it to you because I believe it is true that the Creator did this. It makes sense to me. This Geezus showed by His life how the thoughts of the Creator were pleasant and caring to all people and always had been. Geezus gave out compassion and kindness the same to everyone He met. He told people the truth about the Creator even though it was sometimes hard for them to hear. He pointed out how belief in an angry God was to be set aside. Many could not understand because they were deceived by fear and insecurity. His words were life and truth, but they made many people angry and so wanting to kill Him, which He let them do in time. Little did they know that even in His being killed He was showing this infinite love of the Father God. He came back to life to show that even death cannot separate us from Creator's Love. Even if a person does not understand this love and cannot accept it as true, this does not change His Love. Someday every tribe and person will see this to be true. It may be after they pass beyond the clouds of this life that stop their sight, but it is true that every knee will bow down and every tongue profess that Creator holds us all in His arms and has shown us this in Geezus Yeshua . It is okay if a person does not believe this, but it is a better life if we understand that we are loved. This understanding gives us freedom and purpose. Knowing of this unconditional Love quiets us down so we can enjoy the existence we have been given.

This is Manidoo Gizisoons (Little Spirit Moon), the moon time in which many celebrate the Little Spirit that came from the Everlasting and was really the Great Spirit covering Himself with the skin of a man.

Love,
Mishomis (Grandfather)

Letter Fifteen
Gichi Manidoo Giizis 1932
(Great Spirit Moon)

Tulugaq Kagagi —

I will write a little more of why knowing the love of Gichi Manidoo is good and how this can affect the big world. This is something that I am compelled to talk about. The Teacher inside is always pushing me to tell about this good news because it is the beginning and end of all-knowing. Nothing is more important for our lives and for peace in our world. We must see the world through this law of the Spirit, the law of love.

We clearly see how fear and mistrust stirs up the world. If we are judging through this law of fear and death, we are swift to shed blood. About sixteen snows ago in the European country people killed each other more than the number of stones on the shore of Reindeer Lake. This was the most ever killed at one time in the history of all people who waged war. They used iron machines with engines that had only the purpose of destroying and killing. They used poison gas and any other way they could because they were fearful and hated and were so divided from each other. They dug out trenches in our Mother and lived and fought in these. When I was a very young child the Americans fought each other in a big war between the north and south. This division in the family of man is not just seen in great wars but also in families and in anger between individuals. It is seen between different religions, too, and each one thinks their god gives them the right to be divided from others. Many use their god, which is made in their own image, to justify their insecurity of other peoples. They say their god tells them only they are his. It has often been like this with humankind. This is because they do not know the extent of love of Gichi Manidoo and do not believe we are all of equal value in His eyes. When you believe that your brothers and sisters are ranked in value by the Creator as worse or better than you, it becomes easy to mistreat them. When you do not understand how we are all of one Maker and Father and Spirit then it is easy to fear and mistrust the 'other.' The 'other' is a deception and a hoax. We do not see the hearts of our brothers and sisters as being like our heart. This makes us fearful and we think that others may have bad motives toward us. The family of man is made as one body. Does the head hate the foot? Is the knee suspicious and mistrustful of the leg? Does a finger have no need of the hand or a hand not think it needs the eyes? If the hand would poke out the eyes, it is hurting itself as well. This is the way it is when we do not have revelation of our oneness and unity.

Gichi Manidoo, the Great I Am, has made all things one. Just as the Creator is One and not divided in Himself, so, too, all that He has made is unified in Him. It is not possible to break up His creation and say some is not needed or part of it is no good and no longer belongs to God. It is a lie, a deception, to think all is not one in Him. This thinking promotes pain and division in the world. Now, you can think on this with your head for a long time, but in order for it to grip you at the core, you must hear it from the Teacher within through the words of the Spirit. Then you will have some power and medicine to live out this truth. He will show you our unity and oneness with Him and all He has made. When you experience this unity in loving acceptance from forever, the clarity of our oneness with all people and things is seen. Fear flies far away and it becomes a truth deep inside you that the universe is good.

To know this, to hear and see this, to experience this, is to be in a small way knowing the connection with the heart of the Great Mystery at the deepest level. When this is happening you, too, are loving as He is love. You can know that the strife in the world and in our personal lives is because of not letting the Spirit of Understanding move in us. You can know that all will be well. In your own small way you can begin to live more fully human and allow the world around you to be. This is the way of the Spirit. This is the way of the perfect law of love that is the law that governs eternity, for God is love.

One early morning last summer I was far out on the lake fishing. My bait was cast out, but the line in my hand was tangled up. I had to let it sink as I worked on getting the mess taken care of. I worked and worked at it, pulling out more line, letting the bait sink deeper into the water. It was farther down than I had ever let it go before. After I untangled the mess, I was slowly bringing up the line when I sensed a tug. The line was so deep in the lake that the tug was not immediate in my hands because of the stretching in the line. When this happened, my person was no longer aware of the little jiimaan (boat) I was in. I was not aware of the rising sun or the breeze blowing on the water or the time passing. My person was caught up in wonder at this great mystery in the depths pulling at my line. Very slowly this being would let me tease him up from the abyss. Sometimes it would pull away and I could not resist. I was at the mercy of great Namegossika's (trout) influence over my thoughts and over my small jiimaan (boat). Eventually he allowed me to see him. He was the most powerful and beautiful Namegossika I had ever caught a glimpse of. I knew that I could not get him into my jiimaan because of his size. He could have broken my line at any time, but I got hold of the hook with my pliers and let him go. He did a funny thing. He did not swim away. He stayed at the surface by my jiimaan's side for some time. He and I looked at each other in the eye and I told him thank you for letting me experience bringing him up from the great deep. Slowly he turned and swam into the dark, then shortly he came back again as if to say, "You are welcome. Now you know about me. Now you know I am truly here." Then he gave a loud splash on the surface and was gone. I think he weighed as much as your big dog, Dende (Bullfrog). When I come to myself again, the sun had moved across the sky and I had been taken far into a bay of the lake. Because Namegossika had so caught up my attention, it was like I was seeing this bay new for the first time.

This is how it is with being touched by the Spirit in understanding His love and our oneness with Him and with all others. It is a big thing that cannot fully be taken in just like I could not get the great Namegossika into my Jiimaan. It is a deep and beautiful thing that comes up and changes the way we see the world like Namegossika changed my view of the bay that day. Just as Namegossika's presence was true even when I didn't know he was there, so it is with the truth of the love that embraces all things. This reality of our oneness and equality in God is truth, but few will see it until they give ear to the Teacher within. To taste this love is to be set free to live, and to love others and to enjoy your place in creation. Taking time to be honest, humble and quiet will begin to untangle life, so that like my sinking bait, we can sink down into His truth. The Truth then is brought to the surface to be seen and known. It is not a hard thing. My bait sank down to Namegossika without effort when I untangled and played out the line. Look and listen to His Spirit in your heart and you will begin to be aware of His friendship.

When we catch a glimpse of this absolute acceptance by Gichi Manidoo, the Master of Life, it is irresistible and it floods into our being. When a person knows the truth of the One Great Love, they can believe in it and have medicine in their being to live out His love. This truth creates our belief. Our belief does not create this truth.

The power of this Love can come and go in our lives. We are only human. We are dependent on the Spirit for this power at each moment. Don't be discouraged if the medicine of this unconditional love seems weak at times. This is natural in this life because we are easily distracted away from the truth and the power it has. Even when you do not love like the Great Love, that doesn't mean you are not loved by Him. But let the reality of this love and the unity and equality of all people transform your mind. The more you think on it and experience it the more you can live out a life like Geezus did who showed us the Love from Forever. He knew we were all of same infinite value in Creator's eyes. He was loving of all people, even to laying down His life for all who even rejected Him.

As I said at the beginning of this letter, to know this good news is the beginning and ending of all knowledge. This is for each person to have revealed to them by the Teacher. Each person has their journey.

This is the time of Gichi Manidoo Giizis (Great Spirit Moon) and the sun is beginning to spend more time above the edge of the world. We are keeping warm with our new stove that James brought us from Brochet. We have plenty of wood stored up. Adik and I are reminded this time of the year that just as the sun is starting to give more light to the world, so too we give more light to the world as we let our understanding of His love show.

I am going to write no more tonight.

Love,
Minominike Gissis Makwa

Chapter Eight: Family

The earliest I can remember thinking about my birth parents was about the age of nine. I was playing with a number of my boy and girl friends in a partial cave we dug out of a snow bank. At its entrance we had built a fire. One of them made a belittling comment about the skin of our teacher being so light it seemed almost possible to see through it.

The light from the fire tinted the faces of my Indian friends a deep red-golden hue. For us, at that moment, the entire world was contained within the light and shadows of our little cave. Through this light, I sat staring into the faces of my friends and for the first time realized my difference. As if on cue by an unseen director, my friends considerately turned their eyes my direction. Who or what we were and our relationship to one another had never before been questioned. We had always been connected in tender friendship. For several moments our minds were fused in silence on the same thought. Across the light two hands reached for mine, and the voice of one sitting next to me said, "We are proud to be different on the outside, but we're all the same inside. We are one family."

I went home that night wondering what my parents had looked like. I knew they had left this world just after my birth. James and Peepeelee were now my loving mother and father and yet a dawning desire to know my first parents had begun.

Years later, after living in the south for some time, I inquired of the company my birth parents had worked for to see if I could learn about them. Unfortunately, no records could be found. In Minominike's first letter of Onaabani Giizis 1932, he had mentioned that my father had come to this land from England and my mother from Germany. To this day, as I sit here in the cabin of my upbringing, this is all I know about them. Somewhere in the cold of Reindeer Lake, during the spring of 1928, they left this life.

Minominike's letters, in mentioning my birth parents, cause me to look at my own 'earth suit' to see the faces of my first parents. I imagine the same skin tone, eye shape and hair color. I know I carry their image and mystery.

Minominike speaks to me, to all who read and listen, of the honor of being unique and beautiful as English, African, German, Indian, and Inuit, all expressions within the family of man. "We are proud to be different on the outside, but we're all the same inside. We are one family."

Letters Sixteen through Nineteen

Namebini Giizis

Letter Sixteen
Namebini Giizis 1932
(Sucker Moon)

Tulugaq Kagagi —
I must tell about your big dog, Dende (Bullfrog) and my old dog, Willie. Dende showed up at our cabin one day awhile back with James when he brought us the new wood stove from Brochet. We were setting stove up inside when we heard Dende start in with a mad growl and barking, so we looked outside. A Bizhiw (Lynx) had chased a Waabooz (Rabbit) across the snow between the cabin and the river. He must have been hungry to be hunting so close to our place and didn't pay attention to there being dogs around. He was only a couple canoe lengths away from Dende and Willie with his back arched up, growling and hissing and ready to fight. Dende, who is still young, had his hair up and was snarling and thinking he could easily beat up the smaller Bizhiw (Lynx). Old Willie looked at Dende and the Bizhiw and ran to stand behind James and me. Willie had tried to fight one of these guys when he was younger, too, and he learned a lesson that he didn't forget. Willie has seen many Bizhiw and he respects them. He knows they have a right to be around, so he says hello and leaves them alone. They have their ways and he has his ways.

So, Dende is thinking because he is young and tough and big that he will show this fellow who is in charge and run him away. He took off for Bizhiw and the fellow jumped onto Dende's back with his claws digging in. I heard about men who ride wild, bucking horses for sport. I saw some pictures of this once in a book. Dende started to howl and the Bizhiw was hissing as he rode him off toward the river. Dende was spinning around but could not get him off his back, so he started to us for help. He ran right into a stump near the outhouse and the wild hisser flew off along with some of Dende's hair. The Bizhiw ran into the woods and your dog ran the other way to us near the cabin. He was not hurt too bad, but he was whining and spent the night licking his back and sides. Willie seemed to be pleased with the whole thing and had a look on his face like he was laughing at Dende for trying to be showing off his power because he is big and strong. I think Willie was happy the way it turned out. James and I laughed about it and told Adik later on. She was napping through it all.

So, I thought I would tell you this because when I was a young man I was bigger than most my age. I would not say I was proud of my size, but I did think I was something. One time, when I was down to the school in south near Winnipeg, I didn't get along with a smaller fellow. He was a

Scottish guy with red hair. I was not letting Spirit guide me in my thoughts about this. A day came when I tried to put the smaller fellow in his place. We had a bad fight when he disrespected my long hair and I made a joke about his hair color looking like a monkey's ass. We had just seen drawings of a monkey from somewhere with a red ass. When we were fighting he got on my back like the Bizhiw did with Dende and was riding me and hitting my head. I was spinning around and shaking, trying to get him off and we both fell into a mud hole just when some teachers came to stop us. I still feel bad about this so many snows later. He broke two of his fingers because he hit my head so hard with his fist. I didn't even get one punch in.

When we are not letting the Spirit be heard, other voices will take over speaking. Sometimes they make us feel shameful or lowly and sometimes they will be leading us to be self-centered and prideful. To be listening to the deception of the lowly voice will prevent us from being whole and strong of heart. If we are listening to the selfish voice we will have false center of thinking. We will promote our well-being at the expense of others and we can easily cause pain to others and ourselves. This is something each person must learn for their own knowing. I didn't think so at the time, but after a long while I heard the Teacher speaking this lesson to me so I would learn even from this fight that was a negative thing. The Spirit said the red-haired Scottish fellow did me a favor when he was beating this into my head. I saw that I was following other voices that were not in line with the Spirit and His law of love.

It is often hard to hear His voice within because there is much distraction. He whispers truth and love and acceptance to everyone, but the voices of the world shout Him down. You can tell a false voice by the turmoil or unsettledness or fear it causes. So, as best we can we try to quiet down these other voices and listen to the Spirit. His ways will bring less selfishness and self-promotion to our being because we will understand that Eternity embraces us no matter what comes our way. Out of the strength of knowing this truth we can walk a path of more rest and peace. We are settled in ourselves as we settle into His Spirit. We can better direct our footsteps on our journey with the light of His words shining in us.

So, maybe Dende is a lesson for us in that he was hearing his own strength and power tell him what to do. He had not yet learned to listen to wisdom as Willie had learned through his life. There are many lessons that we learn this hard way. It seems to be the way of life.

As I have finished in writing this, Willie has come over to me from his bed near the stove and is asking to have a piece of dried meat. This is his custom when it is cold outside. Just before we go to sleep for the night he wants a treat and to be let out to visit his favorite rock and do his duty. When it is warmer, he sleeps outside. I think your Dende will grow up like my Willie to be smart and wise, too.

Love,
Minominike Gissis Makwa, your Mishomis (Grandfather)

PS—I have gotten out of bed to add this to the letter because I have written about violence. Sometimes in this life there seems to be no choice but having to use a violent way to protect the innocent ones. It is a tragic thing, but people often refuse to listen to the Spirit, and in cases where there are innocent and weak to be protected, it may be necessary to fight the attacker with the right amount of violence. I don't know what to say about these situations, but the Creator obligates us to protect the innocent and weak. This has always been a hard thing for me to think on and I don't have full understanding with this.

Letter Seventeen
1—Onaabani Giizis 1932
(Hard Crust On Snow Moon)

Tulugaq Kagagi —
Father Engolf, from the church, was out to visit couple days ago. James and Peepeelee sent you along with him so you could stay with us awhile. You rode on his toboggan and he also brought some pickled herring in a jar for us from the Hudson Bay store. I love this little fish from the ocean, but Adik curls up her nose at it. Father Engolf has been at the mission long time and is a European German man. I think your birth mother was German and your birth father from the English. During Onaabani Giizis he comes early morning when the snow is hard and easy to walk on. He stays all day and waits for the snow to freeze back up at night before heading back to Brochet. You will probably remember him when you read these letters sometime. He knew of Adik's heart attack and wanted to see how we were doing. She has been doing well, although her shoulders pain her. This is because of her heart.

Father Engolf is not like some other priests and ministers. I told him my story some years ago, about the time I was at the school and seminary in south and how I had to leave that place and come home. This is in one of my first letters to you written in Manoominike Giizis 1931 (Rice

Gathering Moon). I told him how the teaching was in conflict with the Voice of Spirit within me and about how Gichi Manidoo has embraced all people whether they know it or not. Just because a person is not understanding of the great love that covers all doesn't mean the Creator, the Father of all, is not loving of them in their ignorance. Who are we to judge why they do not hear His voice? I spoke to him story of how Great Raven redeemed the Light of the World and everywhere there is some light because darkness cannot overcome light. On one of Father Engolf's visits, he said that after many years of thinking on these things he, too, came to understand the sweeping love of God for everyone. No matter how they act or what they believe or where they live or the level of their understanding or their past or the color of their skin, the God of the universe has only One Family. Someday when the fog that impairs our view of the kind face of God is removed from our lives and we pass into the presence of Gichi Manidoo, every eye will see clearly and every tongue sing happy songs of the truth of this One Great Love.

I am writing you this letter because you may someday be taught things that are not the Great Truth. Sometimes a person's instruction in religion can be a loud false voice. It claims to speak for the Creator, but He can speak for Himself. You may find that religious instruction is contrary to your heart. If this occurs, you should pay attention to your heart and see if what is being spoken there is not a higher way than your instruction. When there is this conflict, it is usually your heart that knows best. People get taught a false way and then this is passed on many generations. The mis-understanding becomes so strong that people are unable to fit the truth into their mind even when their own heart is whispering truth. Many say they speak for the Creator, but you should listen for Him to speak for Himself. Listen to hear if what is told you and what the Teacher within says are in harmony. If your heart does not sit right or yearns for something that is closer to the truth, it knows about the Law of the Spirit of Life and Love, then you should question their teaching. This is not a disrespectful way toward people, but a higher way of honoring the Spirit who resides in your heart from the beginning.

You may be taught that in the Great Book of Truth it says the heart is deceitful and bad and cannot be trusted. Those who teach this do not understand the same Great Book of Truth also says that the Lord of Creation puts a new heart into people. A heart that is soft and good and not in darkness or hard like a stone. It is a heart that is connected to Wabun Ahnung (Morning Star), the Eternal Light. The Book says He has poured out His Spirit on all people. Not a few, but all. So, Tulugaq Kagagi, do not be fearful to listen to His Spirit who is speaking in your heart. Remember too to still consider those who think otherwise with kindness. Show them this Light and they will begin to consider its truth because their own hearts know it and are whispering it.

Since the time that Father Engolf visited to speak of his coming to understand the universal love of Gichi Manidoo, many people in Brochet have found more kindness for others and they have a peace. There is less bad judgment of one another. This grows out of knowing that there is no fearfulness of God because the people know His kindness and that they are all equal and loved as sons and daughters. It is good to see.

As we always do when he leaves, Father Engolf gives a blessing to Adik and me with his holy water and I burn some Gisheekandug (cedar) and let the smoke cover him. We are brothers and one with the Great Mystery and this is good.

Love,

Mishomis Minominike Gissis Makwa

Letter Eighteen
2 —Onaabani Giizis 1932
(Hard Crust on Snow Moon)

Tulugaq Kagagi —
This is moon when you came to live with James and Peepeelee. It was a bitter and sweet time. This is the season your birth parents were lost to the lake through the ice and was a tragedy for many. James and Peepeelee were friends of them. Peepeelee even helped at your birth. You were a little fellow. Not as big as most when born. A few days after the drowning tragedy you were brought to James and Peepeelee. You were about 3 to 4 moons old. So the bitter was made a little sweet with your presence. Soon after you came to your new cabin we had a ceremony for thanksgiving over you. Father Engolf, he baptized you when you were born, was there and brought a paper saying he approved of your new home. He also prayed thanksgiving for your new parent's happiness and for their wisdom to not be getting in the way of what God wanted to do in your life. He put his holy water on James and Peepeelee and asked me to burn Gisheekandug (cedar) smoke to cover them too. This is called smudging. This is our custom when Father Engolf and I are together. I told you this. We did same for you, and with my feather from Kinew (eagle) I brushed four times over your little sleeping person to show that the Spirit never leaves us

alone and is surrounding us. Even when we are orphaned, He is still with us as our "true" Father.

It was at this time that it came to me you should be called Tulugaq Kagagi. This is Raven Raven in Inuit and Anishnabe tongues. The name is to honor the blood of both Peepeelee and James. He is Cree/Ojibwa and she Inuit. It is also because you may be thinking you were alone in the world and Ravens are never alone. You will never see a solitary Raven abandoned in the world. This is a truth picture given to us to show us that we are never alone, for in our hearts is a friend that always sticks closer than even a brother or sister. He is the Spirit of God who has many names. It was shown me that Tulugaq Kagagi also is a picture of the two worlds you will live in. You were born a white boy whose ancestors came to this land with different ideas, but you would be raised in a home of the people who have always lived here. So, Tulugaq Kagagi is a name given to you by the Creator through my mouth.

One day, when I was told to write you these letters, it was shown me that this name, Tulugaq Kagagi, would not be the only name you would have. After living for a long time you would take the name Inabiwin Pindig—Inabiwin Awass Wedi. This will be a sacred and personal name for you to use when talking intimately with our Great Lover. This name has meaning of 'Looks

Within — Looks Beyond' because you will come to a time when your heart will be opened to the wisdom of the Spirit. You will start to look past that which is false, temporary and fleeting by looking to the Teacher who was, is, and always will be guiding you, watching out for you and doing a perfect work in you.

This name, Inabiwin Pindig—Inabiwin Awass Wedi (Looks Within — Looks Beyond) is a special name that is close to my heart because it was given first to me many years ago after my first two children, Albert and Angeni, died. I will tell you of this sometime in a letter. Very few people know this, too, is my name. When I was given this name I was told it would be for another person also in the distant future. I believe you are the one and that this name is for you, too, when you can understand.

I am feeling that when the day comes where you read these letters you will know that this name, Inabiwin Pindig—Inabiwin Awass Wedi, 'Looks Within — Looks Beyond', will be for you. It will be a time when you will reawaken to His still small voice.

Do not think anything special of yourself, for all people have the Spirit. Do not let your reawakened understanding make you think you are more loved by the Spirit than another. You will have circumstances in your life that will let you peek through the illusions and distractions and catch a small view of your unity with the creation and Creator. Then Inabiwin Pindig—Inabiwin Awass Wedi must be humble, and in his humility be available to awaken others to the presence of our Lover. To stay humble can be a difficult thing. Do not try to gather others to yourself because you recognize the magnificent truth. Instead, always point them away from you to the Giver of Life.

You will be like the little minnows that tell the people who are hungry and fishing out on Reindeer Lake that giigoonh (fish) is near. When I am in my jiimaan (boat) looking to catch giigoonh (fish) I sometimes see the little minnows jumping out of the water. They are telling me a bigger giigoonh is nearby. Be like the little minnows. They point to giigoonh, something bigger, and not to themselves.

I am making myself hungry for taste of giigoonh. Adik fried up some for supper yesterday and we had our fill. We always love the leftovers just as much. They keep tasting better and better as time goes by.

Love,

Mishomis   Minominike   Gissis   Makwa
(Grandfather Rice Moon Bear)

Letter Nineteen
Iskigamizige Giizis 1932
(Maple Sugar Moon)

Tulugaq Kagagi —
It is morning. Usually, I have written at night. I am going to start this letter by writing a prayer I often say to start my day. It is good to set our mind on things of the Spirit early in the day before we become caught up in other things and time flies away from us. It is a truth that to do this sets us in a good way to enjoy and accept what the day has for us.

˙ — — — ˙

Good morning Lord of the Creation, my Maker and my Friend. A new day is set out before me. It is another day I have been gifted to live. I lift my face up to the sky above for the blessing to know that You, Father Creator, are with me. I bow my face down to the earth below for the blessing to know that my Mother the earth cares for me.

My Unending Friend, give me an open heart having gratitude to receive whatever gifts You have for me today. I let go of my past and what has gone before so that I can be open to reach to my future in this one more day that I have. Help me to find those things I am looking for but also help me not to be closed up from discovering things I do not expect.

I wish to know and experience You walking with me on today's new path. Help me to be mindful of Your desire to touch the earth and all beings through me. Help me to understand Your happiness with the earth, with me and with all people. This understanding helps me be more fully human. I know you as a friend that lays down everything for the one He loves. I am humbled by Your love.

I know that I do not have to be religious or do anything to prove my worth to You. But, I also know that unless I set myself to desire You and to watch for You, I may miss Spirit with me in this and every moment. Unless I look, I will not see. Unless I listen, I may not hear. I desire to feel You, so I will reach out for you. I come to You, not to twist Your arm, but to taste and smell Your truth and experience my oneness with You. There is power in this.

You have given me Adik, children, grandchildren and even great grandchildren— even one who is a little gift from our white sisters and brothers. Through the western door You have called many of my family to be with You. I am the oldest of my family and will soon see the door opened for me. Assist me to honor those who have gone before and to consider those who are to come. And, since I am still here, I believe You have a purpose for me on this day and I accept it.

There is One who must be at the center of my being. This is You. Help me not to put things I own at the center, because my things are not the source of life. Help me not to put myself at the center, because I am not the source of life. At my center is You. You are like the river near our cabin, always fresh and flowing and giving life.

I wish to become a willing person, not a willful person. Source of Life, I let You aim my feet on my journey today. I have not been given many answers to the questions and mysteries of life. I do not need to understand everything. I do not need to control life but be willing to share in the flow of life that is happening around me.

Help me to bring comfort to Adik when her heart pains her and use me to bring goodness to James and Peepeelee and little Tulugaq Kagagi. Guide my hands to help our old dog, Willie, recover from his broken toes he got caught in a trap.

Thank you for the red sunrise peeking through the eastern window of our cabin. It is making the frost sparkle on the glass and is nice.

This is my prayer. I believe it is You who are praying within me and so it is in you that I pray. I have set out ahsayma (tobacco) with this

prayer as You have directed the people of this
land to do. It is our way, my way.

- —·—·

This was a long prayer this morning. Adik is
waking up and is wondering what I am doing
over here by the window. I must go and put wood
in the stove. It is cold in the cabin this morning.
I can see my breath.

Love,
Mishomis Minominike Gissis Makwa

Chapter Nine: Prayer

The openness, sincerity and power of the prayer I had just read was tangible. My eyes filled with tears at the selflessness expressed. Thanksgiving, desire for compassion and patience, and above all, a longing for the ability to be loving, fully human, an expression of His Love, was at the heart of his words.

How often I had prayed out of obligation, out of duty. After all, I was a pastor, the representative and petitioner for members of my church. I was liable to pray. Didn't God and man expect it of me? But this prayer was a conversation between friends, a desire to know one another more deeply. It was based in intimacy, not duty; in yearning to touch and be touched. It was a smile and embrace. A kiss.

Yes, its simple beauty touched me inwardly, but my tears were because I realized what I was missing. Duty, obligation and mandatory performance had turned intimacy into mere association, a marriage of convenience without feelings.

The Spirit was exposing my poverty through these letters. Yet, within this revelation of poverty lay the catalyst to riches. Nothing is of more worth to the human experience than the embrace of love, especially the love of eternity. As I sat staring at this letter, I felt His arms around me, as I hadn't in many years. The Teacher within is more than guide and confidant. He is Lover and Friend.

Letters Twenty through Twenty-Three

Waabigwanii Giizis

Letter Twenty
1—Waabigwanii Giizis 1932
(Flower Moon)

Tulugaq Kagagi —
Reindeer still has soft ice on it. People at Brochet are waiting for first airplane to land on the lake, but the ice puts a stop to this. Also, too much ice to use jiimaans (boats). No blossoms of flowers either. Spring is later, but is coming.

It is a while since I last wrote. I said in the last letter about Willie's broken toes because he stepped in a trap. They were not healing up and were infected. He is along in years. I had to cut two of them off. He was not a happy fellow. I took him to James and Peepeelee to help in holding him down. I used a large knife with a hammer to chop his bad toes off. He only made one yip and tried to escape, but we held him. We put red iodine medicine from Brochet on the wounds and clean bandage. He walked around with a limp for couple of weeks. Adik said he walked like I do. (I broke my ankle when I was young. Maybe when I was only nine-years-old, I caught it between some big rocks and fell.) So, he is fine now and a person can always tell it is his track in the mud or snow. Now he cannot get away with mischief anymore because he has a strange track and we will know.

Do you think we should change Willie's name? I read a book, years ago called Moby Dick. I told James and Peepeelee and Adik about Captain Ahab in that book who hunted whales. He had a peg leg because he lost his real leg to a white whale named Moby Dick that he was trying to kill. Do you think Willie should now be called Captain Ahab?

Here is what I was thinking about today.

I have now lived long enough to see changes in the person I considered myself to be. It is clear to me, after such a long time, that my path of life has moved from trying hard to be somebody to thinking that I am nobody and now to seeing that I am really everybody.

This sounds odd, but I will explain. When we are younger we are thinking about ourselves and what we can get out of life for ourselves. We are too much at our center. We have a need to make a name and establish our own person's uniqueness and importance. After a while we get worn out giving all this effort to looking for ourselves and to creating our name and image. Life brings us to this tired place where we give up on trying to control how we feel about ourselves or how others see us. We must get to this humble place. We should come to understand that we are not able to satisfy our striving for value and importance and uniqueness. When we are at this stage of life we will see that no matter how much we work at trying to be somebody it will be a false idol of ourselves. We can carve out this image all life long, but it will always be lacking. When we get to this point of realizing in our striving that we are nobody, our Creator can be heard speaking to us of our real beauty and value to Him. Once we can start to drop the tools we are using to carve our own image, He can show us our unique loveliness and value that has always been there. No matter how we see ourselves, He sees the truth of the treasure that we always have been. When we catch a glimpse of this we start to see ourselves in everybody and everybody in us. We begin to know we are all the same in our journey down the path of life and in this we start to understand our unity with all others. We are beginning to know of our dependence on the Spirit and to be humble. We are taking a step to see the world through His eyes.

This was what I mean when I say, my path of life has moved from trying hard to be somebody to thinking that I am nobody and now to seeing that I am really everybody.

I have seen that life is better understood backward, but we must always live it looking forward. We have to trust it to having a purpose that it is teaching and leading us even though it looks like a winding path going nowhere. When we have this faith, we can look backward and see the winding path straighten behind us. You cannot know this by being told. It is a privilege given to experience and discover for yourself. This is for each person to learn at their own time. Some learn early, some later.

So, that is what I was thinking about today.

Captain Willie Ahab is wanting to go out to do his duty and wander around on his funny foot that is missing toes.

Love,
Mishomis Minominike Gissis Makwa

Letter Twenty-One
2 —Waabigwanii Giizis 1932
(Flower Moon)

Tulugaq Kagagi —
The willows have sent out their fuzzy blossoms. Some call them pussy willows. It will not be long before many other plants begin to wake up from their sleep.

When I was little and in the school at Brochet, the teacher would bring in a bundle of willow blossoms and give a stem to each of us. They would let us use special colored chalk and we would make the blossoms on the stems red, yellow, white and black with the chalk. Some we would leave natural. These are the sacred colors of the four directions that I wrote about in a letter last year when the leaves were changing color. These are also the colors of the people of the earth: red, yellow, black and white. So when I was young, this was one of my first teachings by the Spirit of the special differences Creator put into all people.

In the last letter, I wrote about walking the spiritual path. Each person has a path all their own. It is unlike anyone else's path. This is how our Father gifts us all with uniqueness, but still we are like our brothers and sisters. Just like the blossoms coming on the willow. Every blossom is one of a kind, but it is still a willow blossom. Its life has been touched by the noodinoon (wind) differently than every other blossom. So too, will your life be.

I see in my spirit that the noodinoon (wind) will blow you to the south just as I was for a short time at seminary in Winnipeg. But because you are connected by your birth parents to that world, you will spend much time there. It will be a time when you will be given many answers before you will have asked the questions. This can get in the way of the unique path that Spirit wishes to take you on. Sadly, this is often done in the world so that people are squeezed into a common form. This is done because many fear differences and want everyone to be having ideas that are same and be acting same. But, I am not to thinking this is way of the Spirit.

When we are given answers before we are asking the questions, we are being shaped into what the answer giver thinks we should be. We are being made into a reflection of the answer giver. In some ways this can be okay but often it may not be the way or in the timing the Spirit wishes to lead and shape our being. We begin to look to the answers that have been put into our heads before we ask our questions of the Teacher within our heart. We lose touch with how to hear Him, as the voices in our head shout down the still small voice of the Spirit.

Most people feel no need to stop or slow down to listen to His humble speaking because they have too many answers already put into them. These are answers that may be of truth, but if they are processed in the head, before their questions were asked by the heart, they are easily written on stone and our mind becomes hard and may close to other things. Answers revealed to us after questions are asked by the heart, keep our mind open and soft to receive His gentle leading.

What I am writing is meant to lead you to understanding that the spiritual journey we are offered to walk can be stunted if we are judging the world through too many answers given to us before our heart leads us to ask the questions. With too many answers to unasked questions, we then are looking out on the world and judging the world thinking we know its meaning. We are telling it what it means instead of letting Spirit speak to us through it.

No flower on the willow is same. Each is formed in a personal way by the noodinoon (wind) of the Spirit as it wills to blow. If a blossom says to the wind, "I am filled with knowledge (answers) and know what you are doing and you do not need to blow on me," it is putting up a shield through which it cannot be made into the perfect blossom the Spirit wind desires.

It has taken many years for me to begin to have faith that our Father is taking all our life experiences in this world and turning them for our good. He is making each one a special beautiful blossom that will be an important part of the whole willow bush.

Love,
Mishomis Minominike

Letter Twenty-Two
3—Waabigwanii Giizis 1932
(Flower Moon)

Tulugaq Kagagi —
This might be a long letter and may take all day sitting here on our cabin porch to write. It is a good thing to do while the rain comes down. The sky is low with fog hanging in the spruce along the river. It is a very quiet day with only the sound of dripping water from the trees. Your dog, Dende (Bullfrog), has been here a couple days and is now lying on my feet. I only have my socks on. So, my feet are nice and warm, even though the air is damp.

I have been thinking that I will go over certain things that you have been raised in to remind you of our ways when you are older and have gone away to the south for a while. Not all the ways of the Ininiwok (people) are best, but I will try to tell you of good and important things of the people. There is understanding that goes beyond this world in many of these things. I have seen a lot of ideas and behaviors from some of the whites from the south when I have been there. Some of these ways, too, are foolish in the eyes of the Creator. It is true and would be good for all people groups to listen to one that is outside their own people because the stranger may see things more clearly. I think it is this way with what I will say in this part of the letter to those in the outside world. I have learned many good things from these other ways, but I can also see things that are not in touch with the ways of the Divine Being.

The way of unity and respect.

The world of the south has many beneficial things. Our Father has given them the gift to understand how things work and power to describe what they study. They have used this gift to make many hardships of life easier. This is often good. Yet, this power has a danger. Many are cut off in their mind from the unity that we are with all the creation. They are too much the observer and do not experience that they, too, are related to all things that they interact with. They can describe the world but cannot enter into being one with it because they are always on the outside looking in. They explain and name things, but the names stand in their way of being connected to these things. I have seen that these people are not aware of their oneness with the world they are looking at. They label and name things and put them into categories, but experience union with nothing. This way holds them back from knowing of their relationship to all things. They are split off and out of harmony from creation because of their detached observing. This is often true in their relationship to the Divine Creator too. There is much talk of Him, but little connection and burning union with Him. It is like a man and women who live together in same cabin but seldom touch or talk with each other.

Because of this lack of connection, value is given to things only as far as they are useful. The world is seen as a thing to be possessed and used without regard. So there is little respect of creation.

I know a man, John Ivanchuk. He is in this Brochet area for a few years now. He is a white trapper from the south and there are other trappers from the south. John is like many who do not understand their position in the circle of the world. The Great Web of Beings and Things seems to have no meaning for him. He does not know his connection to all things. He sees Ahmek (beaver) as being here only for him to get rich. John traps with no regard for the young or future and takes every Ahmek (beaver) he can. He does not leave the young or repair a lodge or dam he breaks down to get at them. Ahmek has been dishonored and is now withholding himself. Today there are so few Ahmek that the government is making a law to stop trapping and taking of other relations that have fur.

Our people have lived here from the beginning and always taken Ahmek. We treated him with respect like all the other dwellers on the land and so he was willing to give of himself for necessary needs of the people. We always tell him thank you and we honor his sacrifice by giving his spirit time to leave his body and find its way back to his kind. We do not willingly waste any part of the gift of any of the beings that give themselves for us. There is never a boasting over the killing of an animal because it is the mercy of the animal toward us that causes him or her to give themselves away for our need. I have heard those from the south speak with undo pride over their kill or trapping. They are not understanding that they are dishonoring the Spirit of Creator, Who is in all things.

All this is because they believe they are separate from things that are outside of themselves.

Tulugaq Kagagi, you must live and teach those around you of our unity to the creation and with Creator. Every day we see this pictured for us in the sacred design of the universe and it was shown to us by Geezus in His life and giving of His life over all the creation. His love was shown to extend to all beings and things. Knowing this truth will help people to be at peace and not be driven to amass more than they need.

They will begin to respect our relation in the hoop of the world.

I will come back to write more after Adik and I eat some oatmeal. Peepeelee gave us a box from the store in Brochet. It is very good with a little brown sugar.

I am back from eating. I am really full. Adik gave me so much oatmeal my stomach is puffed up like I might come apart. Maybe I should open my pants a little while I sit here and write. It was so good with the brown sugar.

You have been brought up in the way of the Ininiwok (people) and you may slowly forget some things after much time in the south, but truth will never be lost from you. These letters will bring them back to your heart and mind.

I wrote about guarding against seeing the world as being a separate thing apart from you. This is easy to do. You should speak to the Maker of All Things every day and He will help you see the strings that connect us. It is a spiritual and physical connection. Every strand in the Great Web of Being and Things has a dignity that reflects the Creator. Keep the union of this web intact in your heart and the Teacher within will be able to speak more clearly.

The way of watching for the sacred.

Here is another truth from our ways you must keep close to your life. It is the way of listening to the sacred and seeing what may be holy. It is connected to what I have written about not separating yourself from the hoop of the world and by this, deceiving yourself into thinking you are disconnected from the love of God.

The sacred can be present in all things of life. Spirit may speak His guidance or His love for you in the simplest of ways. As I have written in my letters, seeing Raven flying in the sky, ashes in a woodstove, a feather from Wewe (goose), knowing a warm cabin, having a dream, walking on stones by the lake shore, a long string, seeing leaves fall, being naked, Maiingan (wolf), Makwa (bear), Kinew (eagle), reading the Book of Truth, Ahmek (beaver), Gichi Sabe (great man of the forest), Mashkode Biziki (bison), Mikinaak (turtle), catching a big Namegossika (trout), seeing Wabun Ahnung (the Morning Star), watching Giizis (moon), even being in a fight with a small red-haired Scottish fellow—all these things can carry a sacred message to you. Whatever is common in the world you are living in can be a thing that is sacred which will speak to you. The voice that is heard without words inside your being can speak through all things making them sacred. Listen to this Eternal One.

It is the word of the Spirit and is light for our path.

So, be aware not to divide up your world into the parts. There is not you and the out there. It is one. It is not you and the other. The Great Mystery is everywhere at all times holding all in one single embrace. You are never hidden from or can you hide from the Everlasting One.

The way of freedom.

In our ways, you do not own anything. You are given a privilege to care for things in your world. You may have a family someday, but it is owned by God. You are only caring for it. You may have a jiimaan (boat), but the jiimaan is made from the tree. Who made and owns the trees? You see it is a gift for you to use and care for. You may have a body, but you do not own it. It, too, is a gift that will someday return to the Gift Giver. He made it from the flesh of our Earth Mother. All is gift to be thankful for but not possessed with tight fist. To be a tight fisted possessor is to consider yourself in full control. If you will be one who hoards the gift of life you will not be free and you will be burdened with concerns. It is much easier to let the Lord of All the Earth be the owner of our lives. Let Him determine the things of His we get to use and appreciate for a short while. In this is much freedom.

The way of restoration.

In our ways, in the eternal way, all are one family. When there is harm between people in this one family it is not necessary to harm back to bring justice. We would be bringing more harm to the one family and therefore to ourselves also in doing that. What is necessary is for there to be bringing together again of the ones involved. Punishment for sake of revenge cannot accomplish this bringing together. This revenge is done often in the prisons of the south. We must act as our Wise Father acts for reconciliation. We must try to fix the break in relationship in this way. There is to be understanding of the harm done and the pain felt. Without knowing the shame of the action, there can be no regret. But without mercy, there can be no justice. There is to be sorrow for harm, and if possible, restitution, and there is also to be forgiveness and eventual letting go of being offended. This is the purpose of our healing circle where offender and offended are heard within the family. Time is important part in the healing. Maybe a punishment is proper for those involved, but only if it helps with bringing back relationship. Reconciliation is our way. It is the way of God. If there is refusal on either side for bringing together, then the wound is not healed for the one refusing. If the offender refuses, they will be struggling on with their sickness. If the one harmed refuses, they will not be rid of the pain or anger until it is healed by forgiving. Time is important and with the Spirit's help all can be made whole again.

This way is shown by the words written in the Great Book of Truth. It is pictured for us in way Geezus lived and died and forgave all. He showed us this holy way of the Eternal One. This is a truth that when grasped can open our lives to realizing the love of God which is always being given out.

The way of the community and family.

In our ways, children are responsibility of all the Ininiwok (people) of the community. Just like you are being taught to view all your elders with respect as toward a parent, so all elders know they are to love and teach you as their own child. Whether a young person or elder, all are children of our one Mother Earth and one Father God. We can say that Mother Earth gave us birth as our One Father God, in love, called us out from her. All have come from the earth, from the life giving humus, which is why we are called humans. It is like we are all really brothers and sisters of this one family. Some are older and so must look after the younger. It is good to have understanding of community this way. Brothers and sisters helping and caring for each other.

Communing in unity makes community. Respect this. It can help bring value to each person as they know in their own way they are able to contribute to the welfare of the whole group.

Everyone has a critical part and without everyone giving of their personal selves something might be missing. Everyone has gift to bring to the rest. Some are gifted in creating things. Some are good as teachers, or looking after equipment, or helping others, or governing.

Here is example showing how each person is needed in the success of community and parenting. I have a man friend who is possessing some likeness of women. You may remember Lawrence, as he is often visiting you. He is very good with you. He is special and respected among our people. He is bridge between male and female qualities. Lawrence has very much insight into relationships and is blessing to our community of people. Lawrence is a powerful person yet being very tender. He is a good picture of traits of the Eternal One, powerful like a man, but tender like a woman. In the south, sometimes those such as Lawrence are made to be put outside the people and must not be who they are. This is wrong. Those like him are a distinct gift to the people. The community of people in the white world are denying of God's ways in this matter. Those like Lawrence are created for a special purpose on earth. Without ones like Lawrence our community would not be whole. He is an example of balance for all.

So, Tulugaq Kagagi, remember, within the community all Ininiwok (the people) are brothers and sisters. All are parents and, at same time, all are children. Each is sent to fulfill responsibilities only they can do. All are to be caring for all others and contributing from their personal gifts to the whole. I know this a good way, and is His way, a universal way.

Let me tell you a story that I have heard that shows this truth. One time there was an Asabikeshii (spider) Mother that had six children. She decided to take a short journey away from her home. She called all her children together—Trouble Knower, Path Builder, River Drinker, Skinner, Stone Thrower and Moss— to tell them she would be gone for a short time. Spider Mother left on her journey and was gone for several days. She was enjoying sitting on a branch hanging over a river when Namegossika (trout) jumped up and swallowed her. Back home Trouble Knower knew right away there was trouble. All the brothers and sisters were called together to counsel about what Trouble Knower sensed. They decided to act. Trouble Knower pointed the direction while Path Builder built a path for all to travel on quickly to the river. When they got to the spot, River Drinker drank up all the water in the river and there was Namegossika flopping on the sand. All the family ran out to see and Skinner took the skin off Namegossika so Asabikeshii (spider) Mother could get out. They were all very happy, but just then some hungry Banaysheug (birds) were flying by and saw the celebration. One of them swooped down and picked up Asabikeshii (spider) and flew off. Right away Stone Thrower knew what to do. The stone went high into the sky and struck the Binayshee (bird). It was startled and opened its beak. Spider Mother jumped out. She would have crashed on the rocks but Moss was fast to run over and Spider Mother landed softly on his back. They all ran back to safety of their home. As days went by Spider Mother wanted to give a gift to one child that did the most for her. She found a beautiful round glowing silver stone along the lakeshore. She thought hard about which one to give it to, but could not make up her mind. Finally, one night the glowing silver stone was given to the clouds to hold because she could not decide. The silver stone turned into Giizis (moon), and has been in the sky ever since because Spider Mother realized that the gifts of all her children were equally important for her to be rescued.

So, this shows us that no matter how different each person may be gifted, every person is a key to meeting needs of community and family and has a role to play.

I am going to stop with reminding you of some of the ways of the Ininiwok in the north. What I have written is most important ways. There are many other things, customs and ways of doing. But, it is the things I have written above in this long letter that are holding important truth for you wherever you go.

All day I have been sitting on the porch writing and listening to rain. Dende left for your home after he had his share of the oatmeal with me and Adik. I think I am wearing out this pen in writing so much. Next time I go to Brochet I will see if I can buy one at the store. I will get some nice ink, too. I have been using ink I make from soot in kerosene lamps and the stove. The store ink is much better.

Adik says she wishes to say some things in this letter about history of our family. I must stretch first and rest my hand and then I will write Adik's words for her.

It is me again little Tulugaq Kagagi. Minominike has been writing so much that I thought I never would get to say hello.

My heart is doing better. I get tired easy and have a pain in my arm at times, but I am doing almost everything I want. Even walking more. We will walk to your house maybe tomorrow or next day when rain stops. I can't wait to play with you.

If I could write I would be putting many letters together for you. I must talk to James about getting Peepeelee a new set of cups. Last time we were at the store I saw she was really liking the glass cups and saucers. They had little violets on them. The ones she has are cracked and chipped up. I am going to give this grandson of mine a little money to help him buy the cups for her as a surprise. It has been a long time since fall when he was guiding and made money from the hunters. So, I will help him to buy them. Soon, when ice is gone, some fellows will come up from south to fish and hire him to take them to the best places on the lake.

Minominike read his long letter to me. So I can say a lot of things, too, which I am making him write.

When I was young I knew this tall fellow, the one who is writing all these letters to you. I heard he was a smart one at the school. My friend, Tanis (Little Daughter), told me about him. She would take things to the teacher at the school and she saw him. I had moved near the town with my family and at the end of school day I would go to look at him. I liked what I saw and he talked to me after seeing me there a number of times. Some days I was there, but he was not going to school. He was out trapping or fishing with his friends.

After a year or so this tall fellow went away to the south for schooling, but it was not right for him. He came back and I did not know it. I was at home when my father said we had a visitor. It was Minominike Gissis Makwa and he talked with my mother and father about the time in Winnipeg and how he could not stay and was thinking it was for him to return to Brochet. He did not say much to me on that visit. My mother wondered why he had come to tell them all these things, but she then looked at me and said that this tall fellow probably liked me and wanted to get on good side of our family. That was okay with me.

Minominike Gissis Makwa and I talked often and he was very much liking my eyes and my long black hair. He said so. It is still long and down to my waist but not too black now. He said it was right for him to be back in his home country and with me. After a year we got married. I was about sixteen snows. He was older than me a little. Maybe 18. We lived with my parents for a year and then we lived in a place near the river mouth. I had three children there. Later Minominike and my father built this cabin we are in farther up the river in a warmer place.

There was the illness of the pox and it took away two of my little ones. Our oldest boy, Albert, and little girl, Angeni (Angel). It was a very hard time. Maybe hardest on this big tall fellow here. He left the cabin for almost two moons and only come back three short times to see if I was okay. I understood his heartache because it was mine, too, but he said he had to be alone with it. My mother came and stayed with me during that time. The little ones are buried at the church. In our way, I kept their spirit bundles for a year. Their marker and bark house over the grave is worn down now, but we will repair it sometime this coming summer. Their spirits are in presence of the One that gave them and they are in the love and joy of all who went before.

Our third baby lived out the illness but had scars. His name was Pembina (Berry). He was James' father. He was much help at the church when he grew older and he very much liked to be by himself in his jiimaan (boat) to fish. Pembina was a good father to James, and when James was old enough, he went far north with a missionary and met Peepeelee (Bright One). Pembina was concerned if James marry her there could be problems among the people. Many of our people, and the Inuit too, don't understand each other and there have been evils between us. There was a family talk and Pembina said if it was right with Peepeelee's family, it would be a good thing. Minominike and I said the same and that all the people, hers and ours, would be benefited with this. So next year James went back to far north again with the missionary and Peepeelee's family was happy to see him. After they married, James stayed in the north with Peepeelee for few years and then moved back home with her which was okay with her family. Everyone here thought Peepeelee was a wonderful person and this has made things better with understanding her people. They go north to visit Peepeelee's family now and then. One time one of her brothers and a sister came here. They live in a region near a river called Kazan and sometimes near Maguse and the Hudson Bay. They sometimes move with seasons. The clothes they wear in the far north are beautiful. Peepeelee has mitigwakisin (boots) made of the white makwa (bear).

James and Peepeelee never have children and were together almost twenty snows before you came to live with them. Your white parents were nice people and friends of James and Peepeelee. Peepeelee was assisting when you were born in Brochet. She knew your mother. They liked to have tea together often.

Good night for now. This tall fellow is complaining about getting sore fingers from writing so much.

Love, Nokomis Adik (Grandmother Cariboo)

- — . — .

It is getting dark and, yes, my hand is hurting again from writing so we are going in the cabin now. Adik say she may talk more another time.

Love,
Mishomis Minominike Gissis Makwa

Letter Twenty-Three
Ode'imini giizis 1932
(Time for Picking Berries Moon)

Tulugaq Kagagi —
I am going to tell you something that
happened in Pembina's life. Adik mentioned
Pembina in my last letter. He was our son. He was
your father James' father and our only child that
survived the pox. Adik said he helped with
mission work often and that he liked to be out in
his jiimaan (boat) fishing. I remember the name
of the missionary was Father Gaste that he helped
much. This man was from France. He went north
to the Inuit people, too. Everyone liked this Gaste
missionary. I did, too. So, here is what this son of
ours told us once. He was maybe thirteen snows
when this happen.

He was floating down river near mouth where
it enters Reindeer Lake. It was spring with lots of
water flowing and he was busy looking over the
side and pulling in his asub (net). He didn't
know there was a log from a tree in the water
and when his jiimaan hit it he turned over. He
could not swim good and was fighting the fast
water, but was going under. He thought he was
going to drown and was very sad that he would
be leaving Adik and me all alone with no
children left. As this sadness crossed his mind, it
stopped him from fighting in the water and he

became calm. When he did this he floated to the top. When he struggled, he would sink. When he gave up and was calm, he would float again. As he was floating down river and getting colder, his jiimaan came near him and he grabbed it and was saved. He got to shore and cried.

He told us that in his heart he was hearing Gichi Manidoo speak to him about this happening. He sensed Father tell him that by being quiet in the water he was trusting it and so it could buoy him up. All his fighting and resisting would not help. Pembina said that he learned this is like Father's love. When we are trying to take control and force our way in life we can drown. When we become quiet, the love and care of our Father is given a chance to buoy us up. The very thing that we think we must resist is the thing in which the arms of Creator are reaching out and helping us. It is a thing for each person to learn.

After this, Pembina liked to spend time being quiet every day and listening to the Teacher within. He was a very peaceful person who many of the people came to for help in their problems. He married Onaiwah (Pigeon) and had James. After James and Peepeelee were married a few years Pembina died. This was reason James and Peepeelee move back south from her people in the north by Kazan River, Maguse and Hudson Bay.

They came home and lived with Onaiwah to help her.

Pembina was sort of shy and self-conscious because of scars from the pox illness when he was small. He often was fishing alone and this was time for him to be filled up with the Spirit. His life was not long like mine, about forty some snows, but it was contented even so. I enjoyed his presence especially because he was such a loving person. I miss him still. He spent much time in the love of God, and when you know you are loved just for being who you are, then you are free to love others.

Pembina used to say about this time where he almost drown that it was the happening in his life that most awakened him to the ultimate kindness and compassion of the universe. He did not have to carry much weight of life because he learned how to give concerns to the Strong One and rest.

Adik also say in the last letter about my being alone with my sorrow over Albert and Angeni (Angel), our first children who died. They were older than Pembina. I must talk about this.

I will say I am still with the wound of their passing these many years later. They were so lovely and I can still see them pulling our dog's ears and tail and laughing together. I remember them poking at my eyes when I would pretend to sleep on the floor and playing with Adik in the big rocks by the river and hiding under our bed when they would hear Maiingan (wolf) calling at night. They were about seven and six when they got the pox illness and died two days apart. Pembina got it, too, as I said, but lived. We wrapped up their little bodies in their best clothes and they are buried at the mission in Brochet with their tiny feet to the west and there is a small bark house over their grave.

After this happened, and after the days when their spirits had traveled to go to Gichi Manidoo, I could do very little. I could not stand such a heavy sorrow and did not eat much or work. Our cabin was lacking their voices. There was no power in me to help Adik with Pembina who was only maybe three or four, so her mother came. To this day I am sorry about this but I could not help it and they understood.

So, I painted my face black and went away to a place where I have gone at times since. I have taken James to this place. There is a spring a long day's walk to the north. The water makes a large round pool and is so deep it is black like a mirror. I went there the first time with my father when I was about ten. My youngest sister in our family died a few days after her birth and my father went to this place to offer prayer and grieve. He told me it was a sacred place of our family. A place to receive healing. I felt that I was to go there, too, and Adik said it was right.

I carried only a few things with me. My sorrow was too heavy. I did not even care if I lived. I built a little lodge of willow and spruce on the western side of this sacred spring of my fathers. I put a door in the east and in the west of this lodge. As my father had done, I offered ahsayma (tobacco) and prayer for Adik, Pembina, myself and others four times a day and I did not eat or drink for four days.

On the fourth night I was sensing that I was to drink from the spring and as I did it was like a renewing river of life was flowing down inside me. My heart was starting to heal with peace from the One who cries with us in our pain. I felt the Lover of my Heart say to me that this wound will never completely heal, but He would use this suffering to make me more fully human. I could begin to accept this because I could again feel His love.

On that night I ate pemmican made with blueberries that I brought along. When I woke up in the morning there was fog over the black pool of the spring. I was sitting in the lodge looking into the fog and thinking how the Spirit was so real and comforting to me the night before. As I stared through the fog, I could just make out that a fully black Makwa (bear) was sitting across the spring and looking back at me. Even his muzzle was black like the sacred color of the west with its door to the next life. His eyes were looking into mine and I was understanding what he was telling me. I felt him say that the courage he brings to us to face such hard things in life is really the courage of faith in the Ancient One Who cares for us. He is there for us and will never leave us in this life or the next. He will hold us in our sorrows, and when we cannot go on, He knows our pain and will carry us.

The passing of my little ones had tested my faith that life had any meaning. Maybe all was pointless and leads nowhere. It was as if I was a dead man walking around until this medicine came to me from the Voice hidden within. Through my drinking of the spring and through seeing the black Makwa I was encouraged and felt I was starting to have hope again. There has been no experience in my life to this day that has been a deeper hurting than this. Yet Great Spirit touched my heart and carried me when I refuse to go on. I had been an angry and dead man, cursing day I was born and God who brought me to exist. In my pain I could not understand. But, I was slowly starting to learn He was with me experiencing this pain, too, and this warmed me *again. In a strange way this darkness became a gift.*

I was at the spring for a few more days when I felt I should return to check on Adik and Pembina and her mother. They could tell I was a getting better and encouraged me to again go back to this place. Adik's mother was helping her with her sorrow. Her mother told me that this is the way it is between how a man fights grief and a woman does. Adik needed another women and I needed to be alone. I was respecting of her advice as she was my elder and I returned to the spring to spend many days several more times.

Adik carried two spirit bundles for Albert and Angeni with some of their hair in the bundles and a few other things. She did this for a year and then we buried the hair in their grave.

I sensed the coming of my final day at the spring when there was an understanding that turned itself in my head with these words. "I am giving you another name which will guide you to approach life. I will call you Inabiwin Pindig—Inabiwin Awass Wedi (Looks Within, Looks Beyond). There will be another human being coming in your future that will also take this name at the proper time." I understood that this name was given because out of this time of sadness I was broken down and reshaped like a clay pot is reshaped on a potter's wheel. From this time on I have tried to look within to His guidance and tried to look beyond myself to hear Him speaking a greater truth. This name is not always a true picture of my being, but I honor Him by taking it and respecting its meaning as I am able.

Tulugaq Kagagi, when you came to James and Peepeelee, I felt strongly you are the one to whom this name is also to be given, but only you will know when the proper time is come.

To this day I can see Adik holding little Albert and Angeni to her and feeding them. I can see them sleeping in our bed with us and crawling on the floor with the dogs. I see them trying to help their little brother Pembina walk before he was strong enough to do this. What they are doing now on the other side of the western door, I cannot know, but my heart tells me they are playing in the Great and Beautiful Love.

Love,
Mishomis Minominike Gissis Makwa
Inabiwin Pindig, Inabiwin Awass Wedi
(Grandfather Bear of Rice Moon) (Looks Within, Looks Beyond)

Chapter Ten: Sacred Name

Inabiwin Pindig, Inabiwin Awas Wedi—Looks Within, Looks Beyond. I put down his letter and turned the name over and over in my mind. The letter's account of the circumstances surrounding this name were beyond my experience and understanding. To lose a child, let alone two at the same time, is to experience grief without equal. How does a human being survive after such crushing events? Where does one find relief to merely live, strength to climb out of the abyss of darkness? How does one keep from letting a root of bitterness grow so deep and intertwined that it forever strangles the being it holds?

It seemed clear that the access to healing for Minominike, partial though it would always be, was in the waiting, the listening, and the abandonment of one's own strength in order to be touched and comforted by the One who joins with us in equal, if not deeper grief. It was in the revelation that Eternity cares and will not abandon us, that he, that we, can continue. It was and is only with the invisible touch of identifying Love that such grief is relieved.

I had never known this was part of Minominike's and Adik's life. Was this part of the reason they could so give themselves in love to me and to others? Surely to experience such loss and survive sets one's priorities firmly in appreciation of the value of all beings.

Sitting here in the cabin of my youth, looking down at the oil stained grain of our old table, I felt the presence of these lives gone before. I reflected on my birth parents, pictured James cleaning his rifle and the touch of Peepeelee every night as I went to bed. There was the smell of wood smoke on the jacket of Minominike and the warmth of Adik as I would sit on her lap. Before my mind's eye arrived the dogs that were part of my younger life and my childhood friends of long ago. My heart began to embrace the marvelous worth of all beings. Beautiful life, like the morning vapors over Reindeer Lake, so fragile, passing so quickly. These visions were, in a small way, to know the name Inabiwin Pindig, Inabiwin Awas Wedi — to look within and to look beyond.

Letters Twenty-Four and Twenty-Five

Aabita Niibino Giizis

Letter Twenty-Four
Aabita niibino giizis 1932
(Halfway Through Summer Moon)

Tulugaq Kagagi —
Adik says I have to write a little more on this thing from long ago about Albert and Angeni passing on in death.

She asked me after my return from the sacred spring to write her the prayer that I had inside during my many days away. She knew that in the writing I could begin to tell her of my inner pain. So, on paper I wrote her of the prayer that was in my heart. She kept it for all these years and knowing that I was writing you about these things, she is being very firm that I put it in a letter to you. Here it is from many years ago...

Master of Life, if You can hear me in this place I am in, You must know how my heart is gray because the light is far from me. Inside I am like the big lake with confused waves going in all directions. There is no meaning to my existence. I cry in the night and look for the sun to rise but it always remains dark. I need eyes to see a future because mine have gone blind. I need a voice to speak for me because I cannot say words to express myself. I need hope. I cannot do this alone. I am like dried up lichen on the rocks when the rains have been held back. I am like a dry spruce seed waiting for your rain, but I fear I may never become a tree I thought I was to be. I cannot hear Your voice. Maybe You have never been there. Maybe I was tricked from the beginning, thinking life was a good thing. This goodness has flown away and I cannot know how it will return. Where are my little ones? Are they gone forever? I need hope. I cannot do this alone. Help me to understand this mystery. The moving lights of the northern night sky even do not bring me comfort of hope in a life beyond this one. If only Your sacred fire would flare up inside me again. Can You open my ears to hear You speak, or will the rest of my days be lived in silence? I am angry and You are the One I grit my teeth at. I cannot believe You do not see me or hear me. All I can do is wait at Your door. Please open it and come out to me. There is nowhere else I have to go. The life I have felt from Your face before is the only thing that will save me. I am trusting You are there.

So, this was my words that I wrote at that time for Adik.

I once knew a man who was very sick and a priest took him south to the hospital in Winnipeg. He was opened up and the illness was taken out of him, but the next day he was not better. He stayed in hospital for a long time and slowly recovered to live again. It was like this with the illness in my being after neejawnisug (children) Albert and Angeni pass on. I laid out my being before the Great Mystery and asked Him to cut me open and take away the sickness. He was true and did that, but the time of my recovery went on for a long time. This is what happened to me at the spring and over the years to follow.

It is a good thing Adik was firm in making me write this prayer. It will help you in your times when hope flies away. He remains faithful.

Love,
Mishomis Minominike Gissis Makwa

Letter Twenty-Five
1—Manoominike Giizis 1932
(Rice Gathering Moon)

Tulugaq Kagagi —

It has been a very hot and dry summer. More than I can ever remember. There are even fewer mosquitoes this year, but lots of flies. Fires are burning near La Ronge and Flin Flon. Many trees are destroyed there. I heard this from Father Engolf. He came out to visit and picked you up at your home and we spent today together. He sang me a song in his German that was a birthday song. I think I am eighty winters now. He was carrying you along with his black robes when he got here because it was too hot to wear them and you got tired. He said it was never this hot and dry in Germany where he was born. There are many homes and farms on the grasslands to the west and south that have been abandoned because of this dryness. We must be very careful. Our cabin would be burned up if a fire started here.

We sat out on the porch where there was a breeze and we played a game of dice. Adik won because she plays it much in the winter. I kidded her and said we just let her win so she will not get mad and refuse to make us supper. Then she was really mad, but we had a good supper of smoked kinoje (pike) with some beans and tea. I think the heat was too much for Adik and she went to bed after supper.

Father Engolf and you and I went for a walk along the river. It was getting a little cooler as the sun went lower in the sky. Old Captain Willie Ahab was panting with his tongue hanging out almost to the ground, so I made him stay home. We did not walk fast, but we went all the way to the sandbar near the lake. It was a funny thing we saw there that I had never seen before or even heard of. A cow moose was lying down in the shallow water by the sandbar getting cooled off. We stayed in the brush to watch her. There were two kagagi (raven) nearby and one of them was holding a small piece of driftwood in its beak. The other was talking at him. He flew up in the air and dropped the wood on back of the moose, but she did not move. The other kagagi was making a great amount of noise like laughing. The first fellow flew back and picked up another piece of wood and dropped it on moose again. All the moose did was huff a little and wiggle her hide on her back. The kagagi who was making all the laughing noise kept going on and on and so the wood dropper took another piece above the moose and let it go. This one did not hit the big hairy one, but she stood up and began to bellow in the air. The two kagagi started to fly around her head and torment her like they were going to peck her. She dipped her head down into the water a few times and was throwing water into the air at the kagagi, but then became tired of it all and ran off. We all had big smiles watching this and laughed. I was holding you up above the brush so you could see all this happen. Maybe you will remember this, maybe not. It was a thing that made our hearts happy. I had never seen such a playing thing as this between different relations in all my days. After seeing this I think it must happen between many other creatures too.

Pastor Engolf left you with us for a couple days and from the sandbar he took the path back to Brochet. He was walking down the path and the kagagi started flying around his head, too, for short time. He was flapping his black robe up in the air at them. They were really a pair of rascals.

Love,
Mishomis (Grandfather)

Chapter Eleven: Raven, Raven

In the south I had lived primarily in urban areas. There were the occasional crows, numerous songbirds and chipmunks at the feeders. Once in a while a raccoon family would invade my small garden or a confused opossum would end up under the porch and resist being rescued for forced relocation back to the country.

Minominike's story of the ravens tormenting the cow moose brought back only vague memories of the event. What it did reveal more profoundly, however, was that deep inside I really missed these brothers and sisters in our one earth family. It had been decades since any meaningful encounter with my wild relations. These spirits of freedom, dancing out their ordained roles in the scheme of creation had long ago been life givers, wisdom speakers and beautiful friends for me, bringing amazement and smiles to my world. It was as though they were divine mimes on the stage of creation and I was front and center at the performance. Drama, comedy, opera, tragedy, dance, it was all there, presented before the Author of Creation, bringing pleasure not only to me and the actors but to the Director as well.

I began to think the so-called 'progress' we call civilization too often masks or drives away the divine genuineness and substitutes a virtual reality. As I stared out toward the lake through the ripples of the cabin's distorted glass window I knew that I had for too long been secluded in an artificial world. I had let myself be drawn into the madness of productivity and the distraction of trivial consumerism. I had allowed "a-muse-ment" to impede my ability to muse. The complexity of my life had isolated me from Creation's divine communion. These ripples in the glass through which I was staring spoke to me in allegory—it was difficult to see clearly through the distortion of a distracted life.

Inwardly I craved the simplicity and clarity of the north. It was essential to bring the voices of His performers back into my world. I needed to again take my seat before the stage of Creation and enjoy the performance. This was the guiding voice of the Teacher Within and I knew that someday the call would triumph with my return.

Letters Twenty-Six through Thirty

Manoominike Giizis

Letter Twenty-Six
2—Manoominike Giizis 1932
(Rice Gathering Moon)

Tulugaq Kagagi —
I think I do not know of any nini (man) in my world of the Ininiwok (people) who has lived longer than 80 snows, which I am now. I am baffled why the Holy One has left me in this world so many days. But, there was an ikway (woman) of the Ininiwok, who Adik was close to years ago, that was my elder in years. She passed through the western door almost 90 winters old. She was blind, but never had anyone more vision than her. She was called Agnes.

I have been thinking I must say again about knowing Truth, the teaching of Mikinaak (turtle). This is a short reminder of the things I wrote during Gashkadino Giizis (ice is forming moon) last year.

You will remember that Maiingan (wolf) is our teacher of humility, Makwa (bear) is teacher of courage, Kinew (eagle) teaches of love, Gichi Sabe (great man of the forest) shows us of honesty, Ahmek (beaver) is our teacher of wisdom, Mashkode Biziki (bison) shows us of respect and Mikinaak (turtle) is the teacher of truth. I have spoken of Mikinaak first and last because Truth is the combining of all the other teachings. To live in Truth is to live by the heart because it is in the heart that humility, courage, love, honesty, wisdom and respect all find their home. It is not the head where this Truth lives, but in the heart. The world of the people of the south, the white world, understands much about how things work and this knowledge of the head is good, but this knowledge does not always lead to the beautiful path of Truth. Without the holy and beautiful Truth that is of the heart, the truth of the head cannot be directed.

All of us live more or less in our heart or our head. Mostly in our head. Because I talk much of the heart in my letters, I am not saying the head is to be put aside. I am saying that the head easily pushes the heart to the side and there is no balance.   To be dominated by our head will cause us to wander down the path of control and possessions and the spirit cannot have expression. We will know little of the spiritual path that can bring contentment and peace and meaning. This is how it is with human beings. I have known people who by living so much out of their head have neglected the heart and spent their lives desiring to control their world and chasing possessions. As they have gotten to the end of life they regret this wasted time. It is like vane pursuit of trying to hold wind in their hands. This is a struggle we all must be aware of. The spiritual path is a narrow road, yet it leads us on a beautiful journey.

We do not need to walk this narrow road to make the Holy and Eternal One embrace us and know us. He is always embracing, knowing and loving us. But, if we want to know Him, if we want to have a life of greater rest and meaning, we will have to work to direct our walk according to our hearts and the Spirit Who speaks to us there. We will often have to be at war with the deceptions coming from our head. We must listen to the Spirit's voice and think on humility, courage, love, honesty, wisdom and respect. These are the teachings of Truth that Mikinaak (turtle) portrays to us. Out of the heart will flow abundance of life.

I do not say you can live in balance with this. You cannot! You must put the pursuit of control and possessions in second place. This is the way it is. This is the way that all people must learn. You cannot have it both ways. There will be a love of one and a dislike of the other. The path of Spirit brings life that lasts. Other paths have no true mushkeeki (medicine/power).

Now let me tell you of Geezus and this way of Truth. It is said that Geezus told of himself, "I am the Way, the Truth and the Life." He was saying also what I have told you in this letter. All that

He did was directed by the One He called Father, the Great Holy Being. He heard the leading and saw the path for every action of His life by looking and listening within. This is why all the deeds that He did were covered with humility, courage, love, honesty, wisdom and respect. This is the way of Truth. He lived Truth so He was Truth. Life could not help but run out of Him like water flows out of the springs and into the world. To look on Geezus is to see image of the One He called Father. His path was directed by Him. He fought hard and gave no mind to the things of the world, but looked first to the Spirit and all He needed was added for His life. He was truly a full human being. He was trusting to look within so He could look beyond. He is the true Inabiwin Pindig—Inabiwin Awass Wedi (Looks Within — Looks Beyond).

The time came when this truly Human One was rejected by the people, but even then the way of the Spirit, the Truth of humility, courage, love, honesty, wisdom and respect, was filling Him. He suffered because of this. The people, as people today, could not grasp this kind of freedom and life. They were threatened by it and killed Him. They didn't know what they were doing because they were driven by fear to control their world. They thought they possessed truth but it was a truth coming only from the head and not the heart where the Spirit speaks. The Way, the Truth and the Life was proven to us because not even death and the grave was able to hold onto this truly Human One filled with the Spirit.

Think on this Tulugaq Kagagi. It is the deep thing from everlasting. It is hidden, but is in plain sight. It is a still small whisper that cannot be shouted down and is heard even when your fingers are in your ears. It is the fire that is always sending light to our tightly closed eyes. It is the breath that is blowing between the stars.

Seek first the things of the Spirit and the deception of riches and the need to control will be shown to you as the lie they are. This is for you to learn in your own time. This is for all people to see and become as Inabiwin Pindig—Inabiwin Awass Wedi (Looks Within — Looks Beyond).

Love,
Mishomis Minominike Gissis Makwa

Letter Twenty-Seven
1—Waatebagaa Giizis 1932
(Leaves Changing Color Moon)

Tulugaq Kagagi —
Let me tell you a short story.

There was a nini (man) and ikway (woman) who had a child. This young one was called Wiin Wanendan (He Forgets). When Wiin Wanendan was about six snows old the nini (man) and ikway (woman) had another baby and they called her Wiin Mikwinan (She Remembers). One day Wiin Wanendan told his mother and father that he wanted to talk with his baby sister Wiin Mikwinan. Mother and father thought this was odd because Wiin Mikwinan was too young to speak. Wiin Wanendan told them that he wished the talk to be alone with his baby sister. Mother and father left the lodge but stood close behind a bush to listen. Soon they heard Wiin Wanendan (He Forgets) speaking to little Wiin Mikwinan (She Remembers).

"Wiin Mikwinan, you must help me. It is becoming a hard thing to recall where I came from and who I am and where I am to go. I am traveling and my view of home is growing dim. You have not yet walked too far. Can you remind me who I am and where I came from so that I will not forget and someday I may find my way back to my home?"

When the mother and father heard this it was like an arrow that went deep inside because they too had traveled and forgotten their place of origin and source of who they were.

This is the end of the story. Think on it.

In my next letters I am going to write about the history of the Anishnabe (original people) and the story of Wiin Wanendan and Wiin Mikwinan will open more for your understanding.

Love,
Mishomis Minominike Gissis Makwa

Letter Twenty-Eight
2 —Waatebagaa Giizis 1932
(Leaves Changing Color Moon)

Tulugaq Kagagi —
You are an adopted one of the people. My family is honored to have you. I am going to write you the story of where the Ininiwok (people) came from. This is the story of the Anishnabe (original people). Then, in next letter, I am going to tell you of another meaning of this story. In all things around us, all of creation, spoken words and in this story too there is contained levels of understanding. We can understand these sacred things on the surface and we can also understand them, speaking deeper things of life and the Creator. Gichi Manidoo and the wisdom of the Grandfathers is shown to us in many ways. The story is told in the Neeshwaswi Ishdodaykawn (seven teachings), the Seven Fires of the Anishnabe. This is the journey of our ancestors and it is also the journey of our individual lives. You will see this when I explain in next letter.

Here is the story of Anishnabe (original people). I will tell it in a short form because you will also learn this growing up. Many have forgotten, even among the people. You, too, may forget, but when you are older my words will bring you back to remember.

Many generations ago, maybe more than there are days in the passing of one moon, the Anishnabe lived far to the east near the zhewitaganibi (saltwater), by the mouth of the great river that is called today, Saint Lawrence River. It happened that prophets came to the Anishnabe to tell them of things the future might hold. Each prophet is called a Fire. So, first I will tell you of Neeshwaswi Ishdodaykawn (seven teachings) or Seven Fires of the Anishnabe (original people).

Here are prophecies as passed down by our words.

The **First Fire** speaks this: Anishnabe are to travel west and follow the sacred shell to a turtle shaped island. There will be two turtle shaped islands. These Mikinaak (turtle) Islands will be found at beginning and at end of the long journey. There will be seven stopping places of the people on this path of time. You will know the end of the journey because food will grow on the water in the land of the second Mikinaak Island.

The **Second Fire** speaks: Anishnabe will live near a large body of water before continuing the journey to look for the second Mikinaak shaped Island. However, the guiding of the sacred shell will be lost.

204   Touching Spirit: The Letters of Minominike

*In the **Third Fire** the people will again find the path toward the land to the west of their original home and where food will grow on water.*

*The **Fourth Fire** was given by two prophets, which came to the people as one. They told of a time when another people of light skin would arrive. One of these two that came as one said that if the light skinned people come with a heart of brotherhood there will be many wonderful changes. But, the other of these two that came as one, cautioned that if the light skinned people come carrying greed and violence there will be great suffering for the people, the land and all creatures that live here.*

*In the time of the **Fifth Fire** it is said that the people will struggle greatly. There will be a deception that many of the people may also believe in. It may be the desire for material things and wealth that will charm many. It is the lie that material things and wealth will bring the people joy that will be the reason the people could be nearly destroyed from the earth.*

*When the **Sixth Fire** time comes, those who have been deceived by the promise of riches will fail to explain and pass on the way and teachings of the elders. The young will be turned against the elders. Many will misplace their understanding of life given to us by Gichi Manidoo because they* have not been trained up in the way and power of the Spirit. This will cause many to be unbalanced and life will be hollow. During this period the sacred things will be hidden away so that they can be rekindled at the right time.

In the era of the **Seventh Fire** a New People will rise up and seek to find the hidden sacred things. They will return to the elders for knowledge, but there will be few elders that remember the Way of the people given from the Ancient of Days. This time will be the rebirth of the Anishnabe (original people). In this era the light skinned people will have to choose between the path of the Spirit of wisdom, or to continue down the path which has brought suffering to the earth and themselves. It will be a point of turning to the good or continuing in the way of deception and will affect the whole earth.

Now you have been reminded of the Seven Fires, the prophecies given the Anishnabe (original people). Now I will tell you how history has worked this out.

After the Anishnabe heard and had much debate about the prophecies of the Seven Fires there began the great and long migration. Life had been good and many did not wish to move, but there was change coming for all. It was believed that to stay behind would mean destruction, and that is what eventually happened to those who did not move as the Fourth Fire had spoken.

They remembered the words of the First Fire that there would be seven stopping places. The first would be at a turtle shaped island. They searched for this Mikinaak Island and finally a woman, who was to soon have a baby, saw it in a dream. Using the dream as guidance the people found the island in the Great River, St. Lawrence River. Many of the people camped and settled there. After time had passed the people continued the journey and left this first turtle island.

As they journeyed through the lands of other people they were not to war or do violence but only defend themselves justly. A group of people were selected to keep the Manidoo Ishkode (Sacred Fire) and never let it go out. From it, all the fires of the people were started and so all the people were always linked together by the Manidoo Ishkode. These people are known as Potawatomi now. They next stopped at Gichi Ka Be Kong (Great Falls). I think it is called Niagara today.

Their third stopping place was near where the big city of Detroit is. I heard of this when I was in the south. Some of the people were in charge of trading and getting food. These are today called the Ottawa. Those who were to keep the faith of the people alive, were called the Ojibwa. Much time past, but finally the Anishnabe came to the fourth stopping place on Manitoulin Island in the Huron Lake where they stayed and grew together as a group. It was revealed to them through a boy that from this place there were stepping-stones to the west that would lead to the land where food grows on water as the Third Fire had spoken. So, the journey of the Anishnabe continued to Baw Wa Ting (water tumbling over rocks) where the fishing was good in the many rapids of the river. They stayed there and grew in numbers and after a while traded with the French from this place now called Sault Sainte Marie. That means rapids of good Mary. It was stopping place five. At all these stopping places the people were having more children and growing in their understanding.

The sacred shell had guided them to these places but yet they were not at the second turtle shaped island that the First Fire had said would be the end of the journey. So, the people divided into two large groups and one traveled around the southern part of Gichi Gami (great lake, Lake Superior) and the other around the north of this lake and both settled near Duluth. Those that went around the north part of Gichi Gami are those from which my people have come. The area of Duluth was stopping place six. They knew they were near the end of the journey because manomin (rice) food was growing in many lakes.

The seventh stopping place was searched for. The people who traveled around the southern shore of Gichi Gami remembered a large island that was like Mikinaak. They went to the island and put ahsayma (tobacco) on the sand. The sacred shell came up from the waters and told the people this was the second turtle island spoken of by First Fire. Their journey was at an end. This place is today called Madeline Island in Gichi Gami (Lake Superior) near Ouisconsin. It had taken many generations to reach the journey's end. The Anishnabe grew great in number and the Manidoo Ishkode (Sacred Fire) had been carried the full way. The Fire of His Presence had never left. Creator had accomplished this thing.

So, this was the prophecies of the Seven Fires and the story of the journey of the people. There is much more in the story of the journey that I have not written, but you will hear it as you grow. My words will bring it all back to you.

There is a deeper meaning to these things and I know you have ears to hear it and a heart to understand. The deeper meaning is that this great journey of Anishnabe is also the intended *life path, the journey of a person's being. I will tell it in the next letter.*

Love,
Mishomis Minominike Gissis Makwa —
I am binoojiing (child) of Anishnabe (original people).

Letter Twenty-Nine
3—Waatebagaa Giizis 1932
(Leaves Changing Color Moon)

Tulugaq Kagagi —
You should read this letter with last letter I just wrote. They go together. First one is about the journey of Anishnabe (original people). This one will tell how the journey is like a picture of the path of life intended for all human beings.

Now I will write this thing I have seen in the story of Neeshwaswi Ishdodaykawn, the Seven Fires. There is a picture hidden in the Seven Fires of the Anishnabe and in their journey. I have experienced this in my life. In all things around us, all of creation, experiences, spoken words and in Neeshwaswi Ishdodaykawn (the Seven Fires) there are meanings and truth for understanding beyond the plainly seen or heard. We can understand these obvious things and we can also discover and understand the speaking of hidden things about our life and about the Creator. The wisdom of the Grandfathers and the realities of Gichi Manidoo are shown to us in many ways. Here is the hidden thing of Neeshwaswi Ishdodaykawn.

When we are little we do not see ourselves as separate from our Mother Earth, other people, our Father Creator or animal relations and we are not divided within ourselves. We have not journeyed far from our origin. Remember the short story of Wiin Wanandan (He Forgets) and Wiin Mikwinan (She Remembers) two letters ago? It is short. You should read it again. The beginning of the journey of Anishnabe is like the beginning of our own being when first coming into the world. When we are born, we, as they, have not yet traveled in life. But, we are, as they were, called to a journey of experience that which is intended to shape our being. The Creator calls each of us into existence and invites us on the journey of life. He speaks to our inner person about the mission of life and He invites us to travel. This is like the Seven Fire prophets speaking and encouraging the people to travel through different places until they reached the place intended for them. From the first turtle island they left looking for the fulfillment of the Word.

It is this way — after we are born into the world, we begin the journey in our awareness of our self. We take our jiimaan (boat) out searching for the final Mikinaak (turtle) Island. Remember? Mikinaak's teaching is Truth. The final Island of Truth is where ultimate meaning is found. As we grow up and paddle our jiimaan, it is like we are searching for our home, the Center of Life, the island where we are to live. It is only there that we know fully who we are. Until we find Mikinaak the journey must go on. This is like the people traveling in search of Turtle Island and land where food grows on water.

As time goes by and we grow, there are other islands we may camp on. Maybe fog comes that blocks our view and confuses our direction. We may begin to think, "There is no Island" or "I am the Island." Many forget that they are in the arms of God from their birth. But, their spirit knows and the One who lives within knows the way to the Island of this Truth. He is the compass to Himself. He is the way and truth to the firm ground of life that we can stand on. Many people paddle and row around all their life but give little thought to the Island where their being is intended to be truly at home. We can get distracted or busy. There are stopping places along the way and many people will settle in those places and stay, but there is a final place that keeps calling. We are to keep up the journey going to different islands of awareness and to the final coming home again. It is the purpose of Gichi Manidoo for all of us to paddle and walk the life journey full circle back to our Center in Him, to know life and the Hoop of the World.

Many stop their journeys thinking there is nothing more and they never travel on toward His Beautiful Island and back home. The largest part stop to build their cabin on an island where they believe they are safe. This is because in their journey, fear has captured them and they think they must protect who they think they are at all costs. We all journey with fear, and most are caught up in the controlling of their world fighting to save their false selves. Some think their life will be rewarded or punished and all depends on them because their religions have told them this. It is hard for them to be restful in the journey. Or, they gather possessions and false power around themselves thinking this will bring security and fulfillment. This distraction makes it hard to find rest and joy. They are beautiful to the Creator but their beings are trapped by this lie of insecurity. The freedom of His love is hard to hear. They are their own center.

A few will paddle on to where they are aware they are part of a bigger world and they can give a little more of themselves away to certain others. The awareness of the truth is beginning to open. The Love is being heard. They can see connection to a special group they feel part of. So they are a little freer to give themselves away, but just to that group. One foot is in the Center and one is outside.

A few set out and come to an island of being aware that all people are to be honored no matter what other island they dwell in. These ones are being set free from themselves and are beginning to know the security of the love that asks no questions. They are starting to lose the false self they thought needed to be protected and so are finding their true selves again. Awareness of the power of the Unending Love is beginning. They are becoming open to understanding they are more then only part of a special group. They are starting to give themselves away, and the more they do, the easier it becomes. Striving to save themselves is not necessary.

I am not an educated man. Only Creator knows. In my knowledge I know of only One Who made the full circle journey back to the Center. This was the one and only Human One. Many may glimpse a vision of what it is like being at Mikinaak Island, but I do not know of any others who gave themselves away and were living out from this Center. On this Island of Truth there is joy in all things. There is no fear. There is freedom. There is satisfaction and contentment of life. We are home again. Great Spirit gives us the privilege and honor to go through this adventure in life to seek and find our Island Home. The more we are knowing we are Home, the more we are able to give ourselves away so that others can also see the way through their journey of awareness.

Tulugaq Kagagi, do not forget story of the visions of the seven prophets that came to Anishnabe. It is desire of Creator for you, too. To make the whole journey in your life. Mikinaak (turtle) Island calls everyone. This is the story of our people and it is to be the life story of each person in the world. It is filled with actual places and happenings and it is also a parable of each of our personal lives. Remembering this story will give you help and hope on your journey in giving yourself away. Only when you give yourself away will you truly possess who you are.

I can tell that I am to write more about this in next letter.

Love,
Mishomis

Letter Thirty
4 — Waatebagaa Giizis 1932
(Leaves Changing Color Moon)

Tulugaq Kagagi —
I will now write a little more about this journey of life. You will see the parable better in Neeshwaswi Ishdodaykawn (the Seven Fires) and the journey of the people.

You should read my last two letters to see how all these seven stopping places are pictures of our life journey. Just as there were seven big stopping places foretold by the prophets for the migration of the Anishnabe, so, too, there are seven stopping places of awareness in our passage of life. They are like this...

First — We are born but not yet aware of ourselves as separate from other things. This was like the camp on first Turtle Island and the people did not know what was on the journey ahead.

Second — We become aware of our needs and in this way begin to know we are an individual and apart from other things. We are shaken by the thunder of this place. It is like the stopping place of Gichi Ka Be Kong (Great Falls Niagara) in the story.

Third — We desire to control the world so that we can meet our needs and wants. This is the stopping place of Detroit in the story where much trading occurred. Many do not travel beyond this stage of life.

Fourth — We understand that there are others like us who, too, have similar needs and so we want to feel a part of this special group. This is the picture of Manitoulin Island stopping place where the people were one in their group. Many people find their identity within a group and go no farther.

Fifth — We start to see beyond our group that all people in the world have the same needs and we begin to honor them as being with us in the one family of God. This is like Baw Wa Ting, Sault Sainte Marie where many different peoples fished and traded together.

Sixth — Seeing Creator's unconditional love and our oneness in His family, love grows deeply in honoring all our sisters and brothers with no regard for them returning that love to us. This is like the stopping place near Duluth after they had circled Gichi Gami (Great Lake, Lake Superior) in different directions and where they knew the journey was coming to the end and they again joined together as one.

Seventh — We start to grab hold that Absolute Love has always been with us. We give up our own being and let the medicine, the power of that Love bring us into unending full life and start to bring us back to knowing oneness with all things. We have traveled back to our beginning. We have traveled the great circle. It was from the Eternal Love that we came and it is to the Love we return. This is the stopping place called Madeline Island in Gichi Gami near Ouisconsin. We are satisfied because we are fed by the food that grows on water all around. We have been led to our second turtle shaped island. The journey of the circle, the journey of life, is complete. From our first turtle island, through stages, stopping places of growing understanding, to the truth of our last Mikinaak Island.

The stopping places are stages of awareness in our life. In our journey we can have visions and insights of the final Mikinaak Island. Gichi Manidoo gives us these to encourage us to journey onward. These are states that do not last but let us know that there is higher understanding and goodness and more to fill us. They draw us to the Great Truth. Remember, the teaching of Mikinaak is truth?

Many stay in a stopping place their whole life and do not journey too far. We do not know their story or the type of path they have traveled. Wherever the stopping place of a person may be, it is not for us to judge because if you are still in this world you, too, have a journey to complete. No matter where a person is they are being embraced and encouraged and drawn onward by the One who speaks in the Seven Fires.

Making this journey is our privilege as a human being. Each person walks their own path. Every person is carved-on by different experiences. Each has unique words written on the pages of their book and the Eternal Mystery knows every story. Every happy part, every sad part, every wound and scar, every beautiful poem is known by Him. All our books are cherished by Gichi Manidoo.

You are little as I write these things and you cannot take in what is here. When the day comes for you to read these letters you will understand and see yourself somewhere in the circle and journey story of Anishnabe. You will see that your stopping place is only that—a place from which to launch out your jiimaan for more travel.

Now I will tell you a paradox. It may sound like a contradiction to all I have already said, but it is not. It is the sum of the Seven Fires... We are on a journey and at the end of our walking we are to come to the place where we began and know it for the first time.

So, now in my way, I will send my prayer into the future for the day when you read this.

-—·—-

Prayer—Great Eternal One who lives at once in all moments of all time. I have bathed myself in the cedar smoke and offered ahsayma (tobacco). This is Minominike Gissis Makwa, the one You have called to write these words to my grandson, Tulugaq Kagagi. It is my prayer that these words are Your words. I do not pray that they are loud words in the head, but that they are true and soft words in the heart. I pray that through them this little one will be helped in completing the journey he is on by returning full circle to know the truth of his Being. There is good food and sweet life at Your Island. For him to taste these things while in this world is my desire as I know it is Yours. I will be called to Your side before He is old enough to understand, but I would ask that I could be told at that time that the words have lodged in his heart. Chi Megwetch (thank you very much).

I will leave ahsayma folded in this letter for the day it is opened.

Love,
Mishomis Minominike Gissis Makwa

Chapter Twelve: Stages of Life

The dried tobacco placed in Minominike's letter had spilled out unto my lap as I opened the letter. I stood up and saved what I could by sweeping it off my shirt and pants onto the table. At first it had meant nothing to me. In fact there was a slight irritation at the mess it had made. Now, after reading the letter and written prayer, the ahsayma took on a sacred quality. It was infused with compassion and wisdom of an old man's heart. Searching out every brittle piece, I gently pushed it off the table edge and let it fall back onto the letter. There was a prayer contained in this mixture of leaves, bark and herbs and I desired it to be fulfilled in my life.

At what 'stopping place' was I on the journey? Does life inevitably draw us down the path to know Mikinaak, Truth? How much energy is demanded of us to complete the pilgrimage? How do we make ourselves available to be carried along to our intended destiny? In my heart it seemed clear that the winds and currents of life are intended to present us with opportunities for travel. We are to rest and observe and make ourselves available for Wisdom to speak into and uplift our consciousness. The speed of the journey cannot be forced. The timing may be adjusted by our choices but it is not controlled.

As I pondered these things and brushed the last of the ahsayma back onto the letter, a slight movement drew my attention to one of our narrow shelves near the door. In the shadows I noticed a beetle. Six legs advanced the tiny creature forward until she came to a metal tin holding rifle shells. The tin spanned the width of the shelf. She stared, sniffed, tasted, pushed and caressed the barrier. I could read her mind, "Who put this here? Should I settle down and spend my life in this place? It's warm, safe, and I can pick those crumbs off that table over there when the human isn't looking." After a few minutes, there seemed to be a resignation that this barrier would end her travels. Life was okay. She was in control. She could stay put if she wanted. I turned away and smiled.

In the stillness of the cabin, as I folded up the letter with its sacred ahsayma, I heard a faint clicking and buzzing. I looked back toward the beetle to see her unfolded wing cases. She was testing for flight. Clumsily she lifted off, smashed into the tin and became disoriented among the rifle shells. Crawling to the business end of one shell she launched herself again. Skidding along the wall she finally crash-landed on the other side of the barrier. Righting herself and folding her wings back under their cases she continued to crawl.

In these last few letters, Minominike wrote that he believed everything in the world is teaching and speaking if we have ears to hear or eyes to see. This beetle was speaking clearly. She could have ended her travels at the tin. She could have lived out her life and settled for the comfort of the crumbs from the table. Instead, she had a calling to journey on. Where that journey would take her was a mystery to me and probably to her as well.

Where my journey would proceed, I also could not know. One thing was sure I could no longer leave my wings folded. We are called onward to learn and be transformed by Love and it is most often when confronted with barriers that transformation is potentially the most profound. It is the struggle in the journey to which we are called. It is in the seeking and in the faith that there is purpose and destiny, that existence is revealed to have meaning. We are called to acknowledge this journey and by this, experience the reality of Mikinaak and the now, but not yet, of Turtle Island.

Inner contentment and a peace that passed understanding forced another smile to my face. The crumbs on the table reminded me of the growling in my stomach. It was time for an egg, some oatmeal and then a slow wander along the lakeshore to enjoy this tangible presence of Spirit.

Letters Thirty-One and Thirty-Two

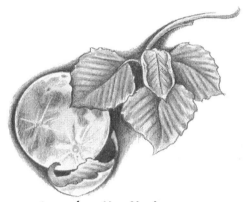

Binaakwii Giizis

Letter Thirty-One
Binaakwii Giizis 1932
(Falling Leaves Moon)

Tulugaq Kagagi —
I want to tell you about ways I use to help me talk with the Master of Life. It is good for each person to have ceremony or a sacred road to help put our mind at rest. Then we can be aware of the Presence. I have a number of sacred things I keep and ways to help me. You should consider some for yourself if you have none. When I pass on I will leave these things in our cabin. James will give them to you when you are older or when he passes on. They have been close to me many years and have given me much help. When you came into my world I added something of you to my sacred bundle. You will see.
Before this, Adik wants to speak.

- — — -

This is Grandmother Adik. It is good for me to write about this now because my tall man told me what he is writing and what I want to say is similar. I have made you a small box with a lid from bark of birch tree and put a decoration of two kagagi on it with gawg (porcupine) quills. It is going to go in this tall man's bigger box with all his letters for you. In my box, I put six little stones. I searched for the stones for some time until I found the right ones. There is a black one, a red one, white and a yellow one. There is also a stone that I put a green circle on and one with a blue circle. The stones are sacred colors of the four directions and the green one is of Grandmother Earth below. The blue one is of Gichi Manidoo above. Grandfather Minominike has stones, too, but you need your own which I have been led to find and to make for you. Keep these because they were here at the earth's beginning and use them to help you in knowing your place in the world and the sacredness of all things. Spirit is in all things and beings. They will also remind you of this country in the north. You will like the pretty little bark and gawg quill box. The gawg gave his body away to us for food and for this purpose last winter.

I am starting to make ziishiib (duck) and manomin (rice). We are all going to eat it tomorrow with Father Engolf and James and Peepeelee. The table will be full with the six of us, maybe seven because Lawrence may come too. He loves to play with you since he has no children of his own. He is a special and good man. He has been blessed with the harmony of nini (man) and ikway (woman).

Good-bye until tomorrow. I will show you the small box and stones but you probably will not remember because you are young.

Nokomis (grandmother) Adik

- —· —·

I am back to write for myself now. Adik wanted me to help with our stove. It was smoking too much. There was a buildup of ash in the chimney.

So, now I will write what I thought would be of help to you someday in your seeking voice of the Teacher Within and looking to Gichi Manidoo. I have often found that my mind races with many thoughts. In order to hear Spirit, to see Face of God with my inner man, to know the Voice, my mind must be quieted of these distractions. It is good for me to use these sacred things and this way helps in my looking to Great Father. You may want to think about your sacred objects, too, that could help. I have a gishkibidagunnun (medicine bundle) that holds these things.

My bundle is made of a small skin from Makwa. I found it in Brochet many snows ago. Someone had disrespectfully left the skin near the store and I searched for the owner, but no one claimed it. So, from being a rejected skin it has now been given a place of honor as my bundle, I have painted the sacred colors of the four directions and green for Grandmother Earth and blue for Great Spirit on the side with no hair. Just like your colored stones that Adik told you about. I roll up my sacred helping things in the skin and tie the ends shut with a leather cord. I will tell you about those sacred things in this letter. My bundle is about the size of our table when it is unrolled.

When I need help to center myself and spend time with the Wise and Living One, the holding of my bundle is the beginning of my personal ceremony. I hold it to my chest and then outward to the sky. This brings me together. It helps center me in my mind and heart.

Each person can have their own way, but this is what I do.

-—First, I hold my bundle to my heart and then up to the heavens and thank the Great Mystery for my sacred things. I breathe in four times slowly to settle myself. I turn to all four directions with my bundle and give thanks in this way...

Prayer—Gichi Manidoo, megwetch (thank you) for these things that help me realize You are with me. I know that You are not hiding from me, but sometimes I have a hard time seeing and hearing You. Open my eyes and my ears with the help of these things.

-—So then, I put my bundle down on the ground and untie it to show the things inside. I roll it out long ways to the east and west and I kneel or sit on it facing the east. I take my small drawing stick from these possessions and draw the great circle of the world on the ground around me and my things. I encircle my unrolled bundle and myself in the one hoop of the world. If I am doing this on my cabin floor, I draw an imaginary circle with the stick.

·—Next, I take my four small pieces of colored cloth and lay them on the ends and sides of my makwa hide in their directions. Red to east, black to west, white to north and yellow to south. I put a small bit of ahsayma (tobacco) in the directions. Using ahsayma is the way of the people for many generations.

·—Next, I take some cedar leaves that I keep in the bundle and burn it in a small shell I have. I send the smoke to all my things. The smoke covers me and purifies my thoughts to help me think in a holy way.

·—Next, I take my stick-self out of the group of things. Does this sound funny to you? I have made up a willow stick to represent me. It is not quite as long as my pipe and it has many items that stand for my life attached to it. I have my face drawn on the stick and where my head and heart would be I have a line from each going up. These lines join together and then point up to heaven with an arrow. This means my head and my heart will be one.

Tied on my stick-self I have a little cloth bag. In it, I have separate knots of hair. Three are of Albert and Angeni and Pembina's hair. Another is Adik's hair. One is Onaiwah's, who was Pembina's wife. One is James' hair and one is Peepeelee's and one is my hair. The last one I have put in there is a knot of your hair. These are the people in my life and they are attached to my stick-self like they are to me.

I have also a folded up page from the Book of Truth in the cloth bag. This is showing that His Words are Spirit and my life source and He speaks to me in many ways. With this are some grains of Manomin (rice) and cedar leaves that remind me that Grandmother Earth is always providing for me.

Around the middle of my stick-self is wrapped some skin with hair of Makwa (bear) like a robe and this is because I am of the clan of Makwa.

Also tied to my stick is one of the small downy feathers that fell to me from the Wewe (goose) when I was at the school in the south. These downy feathers I took to be my instruction to return home. I wrote this to you in Manoominike Giizis 1931 (Rice Gathering Moon). So, I take my stick-self and set it in front of me. All is within the great circle I have drawn and is now centered in the universe and so I offer a prayer something like this ...

Prayer — Here I am Creator, Minominike Gissis Makwa. The one who is learning to call himself Inabiwin Pindig—Inabiwin Awass Wedi (Looks Within — Looks Beyond). I may do many things in my life, but it is my relationship with the people You have given me and with You that is most important. I am being created through these relationships. Help me to be considerate, humble and protective of these special ones and help me to keep You always before me. I am getting like an old stick, but this old stick lives again when You breathe on it and speak to it. Rise up and breathe on me. Speak to me so I may truly live. I trust and believe You are doing that. I have placed myself here within the sacred colors and the four directions. I am the focus of Your eye. I am at the center of the circle of Your Creation and I am trusting that You are with me and in me and surround me.

  -—Next, from my bundle, I pick up my small stones and set them on the four colored cloths with the ahsayma (tobacco) by them. These stones are oldest things on earth and from the beginning of creation. They are for me, a picture of the ancient way of truth that I have been writing in these letters. Truth does not change. It is the firm foundation, like stone upon which the world is built. They are the Grandfathers of wisdom and speak to me that Creator's love and embrace has not changed since the beginning. It is always there. Wherever you go in the world there is stone to stand on even when you cannot see it. It is like the Love that holds up all things. My stones are also different colors like the ones Adik was led to find for you, red, yellow, black, white. I also have two that represent Gichi Manidoo and Grandmother Earth. These two are like yours; sort of blue and green like the sky and the earth. I put these two on each end of my stick-self to embrace me. Blue at my head and green to my feet. Then I pray something like this…

Prayer — I am surrounded by truth and love. You are love. You have me boxed in and I can never get away. The whole universe is filled with Your truth and love. It keeps all things and is always looking out for my good. It is happy when I live in the truth, but sad when I am deceived and in error. Yet, You do not keep track of my failures. Your love sends me trust and hope and is protecting me and shaping me. This love is always kind and patient. It can never fail. These stones are like Your messengers, strong and true. They speak to me of Your unchanging nature and they bring wisdom on my life path. Love is above me and below. Megwetch (thank you).

-—Finally, I will pick up the opwagun (pipe) and put in ahsayma (tobacco). I am only a keeper of this opwagun (pipe). I do not own it. I am responsible for its honor. I direct its stem to the messengers of the four directions, to Creator in the sky and to Grandmother Earth in respect and thanksgiving and I send its smoke into the air. My prayers are carried on the smoke and as I do these things my mind and my heart become more united. I understand more clearly the oneness of all things in the Spirit. Peace comes to my being and insecurity flies away.

I remain sitting and pray and revere the Most High. I admire the hand of the Mighty and Gentle One in my life and in the world. I will make requests for people in prayer and I seek understanding to walk a good life and help others. I will ask for healing of illness for myself and those I know are hurting. Mostly I ask for those who are ill to be lifted high into Spirit's arms to have a peace in the middle of suffering and strength to see one's way through. I send out my prayers for people toward them by waving my feather from Kinew (eagle) four times outward. I do this for each person. This feather is in my bundle, too.

Sometimes my ceremony is short and sometimes long. Time can disappear, but now and then it drags on slowly. Sometimes I am touched deeply and other times hardly touched. It is not for me to question. I know that my way is for me to do often and overall I am helped by it.

Sometimes, not always, I take my sheshegwun (shaker) from the bundle of things and sing a sacred song. Some songs have been given to me by the Spirit and some are very old from Ininiwok (people) of past generations. When I sing these songs, I feel these are with me.

When I am done I touch my head to the earth. I put all my sacred things into the bundle. I roll it up and tie the ends. Sometimes I will take a nap to soak in what the Presence wishes for me, but usually I have energy and want to go about my life. I do my ceremony often, usually every day. It helps me.

I have seen many people in my life that say they are too busy to take time for such things. Tulugaq Kagagi, I make you the promise, if you will build into life a practice of gathering in the mushkeeki (medicine) of the Spirit, you will have a walk that is not so frustrated and complicated. You will be more quiet inside. Find your ways, and when the winds blow, it will be a place for you to run to that will help you know you are being taken care of and will be OK. This is for you and all people to learn.

When I went to the south, I was told some of the sacred things I had taken with me at that time were not good to have. They were different than my things now, but I did not get rid of them as I was told to do by the people there. My things were close to me and helpers for my heart. I knew they were good.

So, I wanted to tell you this. I have other sacred things, too. I do not keep them in my bundle.

Love,
Mishomis   Minominike   Gissis   Makwa
(Grandfather Rice Moon Bear)

Letter Thirty-Two
1—Gashkadino Giizis 1932
(Ice Is Forming Moon)

Tulugaq Kagagi —
Before I write Adik wants to say things again.

- —·—·

Hi, little fellow. Minominike doesn't know what I'm going to say, but I made him promise he would write it like I say it. He has been writing you about his sacred things and I want to tell you about something of mine. I have sacred things, too, but this is from before we married. He knows about this. It is my charm …He is objecting, but I am making him write …When he came back north from the school and then came to visit my parents to talk, I made a charm to lure him to me. I knew he was interested in me, but there were some other girls that wanted him, too. So I made this charm to send power to him to think of me only. Which he did. I carved two little people and tied them together with a thread from a scarf he wore. I took the thread when he wasn't looking. One little person was me and one was my tall fellow. I put us in a little bag with some red columbine flowers and I wore this. It was very powerful. He couldn't resist.

I wanted to tell you this because he thinks it was all his choice to love me, but I know better. I have powerful medicine.

Nokomis (grandmother) Adik

- — - — -

I put down what she said because I promised. Maybe there was some power in her charm, but it was my idea to go after her no matter what she says.

So, I wanted to write to you about another thing I do at times to help me with putting my mind to things of the Spirit. It is a ceremony of purification in the sweat lodge. This will be something that James will show you and you will remember, so I will not give too long a letter about this.

I have a sweat lodge near the river upstream from our cabin. It is a small one. Only room for six or eight people. It is made of willows put in the ground and then bent over to form a dome like the dome of the sky. It is like the shape of the earth and though you only see the dome above the ground it is extending below the ground, too, in an invisible way to make a sphere. In this it is like the world and the universe around it. It is a full circle in all directions. A circle is the sign of complete perfection, like the Creators work of the whole universe. This lodge has four willows wrapped around it from the bottom to the top. I cover it with blankets when I use it. There is an opening to crawl through on the east, but it is closed up when I am inside.

I heat Stones for the ceremony in the fire to the east of the lodge door. They are called the Grandfathers. I usually heat just seven big Grandfathers and offer ahsayma (tobacco) in the fire. The stones will be the messengers. When the heated Grandfathers are placed in the pit in the lodge I sit to their west and I use cedar leaves to sprinkle water on them. The rising steam is my prayer being carried to the Majesty and Splendor above and it is the knowledge and insight and teachings being sent into the lodge. It is dark in this world accept for maybe the red glow from the heated ones giving their understanding. They are the elder Grandfathers and bring us wisdom.

When I am in the lodge alone I face the east to the place of the rising sun and this speaks to me of our Provider's everyday faithfulness. My thoughts are directed to spiritual things during the ceremony. I may smoke the Opwagun (pipe) and if others are there we will pray and give thanks. It will get very warm and is often a struggle to go through the time with the heat. It is like this in life. There is often darkness and suffering, but the Faithful One gives us strength to get through. In struggle we are shaped into something beautiful and unique as the Spirit wills us to be made. It is the way of peace to trust in our Maker during hard times. This is a hard thing to understand, especially during struggles and suffering, but especially in these times we are cared for by our Refuge.

So, the sweat lodge is part of the Way that Gichi Manidoo gave to the Ininiwok (people) in this part of His Creation. These are good to do. They help us to keep the eternal things and our security centered in our mind. They help us join our heads and hearts together in balance as Creator wishes us to be. Other people have other ceremonies and all these ceremonies and the things I do are arrows that are pointing to God. They are always pointing away from themselves and to Him. These ceremonies help us to center down and give the One Who Stretched out the Earth and Sky a chance to speak to us and have relationship. Life can be a puzzling and difficult thing without trusting He is there.

I have been hearing two kagagi talking on roof of our cabin. I must see if they have something to say to me ...

I am back. I think they were making fun of me for sitting here by the window and writing so much. Laughing and laughing so hard that one of them tipped over and bumped its beak on the cabin ridge. So, I laughed at him and the other scolded me saying not to embarrass them or they would drop things down my chimney and smoke me out of my house again. Now I know why the chimney was stopped up. These guys are pushing me. Maybe I will get out my big *giigoonh ahsubbi* (fish net) and stretch it across the trees and catch them.

Don't worry. I will be kind. Maybe just make *kagagis* think I'm going to eat them and then be merciful and let them go so they owe me mercy. That would be another laugh for me.

Love,
Mishomis (Grandfather)

Chapter Thirteen: Sacred Space

Reading Minominike's brief description of the sweat lodge brought back vivid recollections of my first sweat lodge in the north. It occurred when I was about seven years old. Lodges were both a sacred and social gathering.

James and Peepeelee took me into Brochet where a friend had a lodge behind their home. The stones, the Grandfathers, were already heating up under the flames of blazing spruce. A few people stood while most sat on rocks or crude log benches. The fire pit was encircled on the ground by cedar leaves. Clouds of mosquitoes moved about to avoid the shifting smoke. I was the only child there and was called from person to person to be kindly touched and talked to. A few of the dozen or so in attendance had small hand-held drums with beater sticks and everyone had a shaker to use while singing in the lodge. James had made mine from a piece of small antler for the handle. It had a sewn, dried, rawhide pouch stretched between the tines that contained tiny pebbles to shake. One man had come with a pipe and all the women were wearing long dresses.

I was in wonder and a little scared at the darkness inside the lodge. The passionate singing, the sound of a raven, wolf or moose being imitated and the rising temperature as the Grandfathers gave off the heat of their wisdom, created a dreamlike universe in my young mind. Every now and then a flurry of feathers beating the air could be heard as the one in charge waved an eagle wing fan in the heat and spread the incense of cedar around the lodge.

Within the lodge was sacred space where everyone felt secure and could express their needs. A good number of people prayed openly and unashamed while some spoke freely of their shortcomings without fear of judgment. Everyone sat as equal children in this circle around the Grandfathers.

I cannot remember how long this first lodge lasted. I awoke as I was being carried into the house for the feast that followed. Over the next few years, until my departure to the south, I attended several dozen lodges. James eventually made me a small drum and I would share in the pipe of those who carried one.

Staring into the streaming light coming through our cabin window and recalling these ceremonies of youth, I was in awe at the speed with which time had passed and what I had left behind. Maybe it was romanticized nostalgia, but as I thought about the inflexible liturgy, the hierarchy of authority and the rigid formalities of ritual that I now conducted, I couldn't help but desire a softening of these institutional customs. I yearned for a higher degree of intimacy, passion and personal vulnerability among the people I was part of. It seemed the structure of institutional religion, beautiful though much of it was, had a bent toward strangling the fire of Spirit. Ritual, custom, ceremony and liturgy all have value, but so easily become the object and not the 'arrow', as Minominike had said in this letter. All ceremony is not an end in itself, but points to the One that resides over and in all.

I decided that tomorrow I would go into town, look up my few remaining acquaintances and inquire if anyone would once again "pour a lodge" before I left. It would be an emotional time among many people I no longer knew. I also knew that within that sacred space of the lodge could be healing and clarity for a man desiring refreshment within the intimate love of his Creator.

Letters Thirty-Three through Thirty-Five

Gichi Manidoo Giizis

Letter Thirty-Three
2—Gashkadino Giizis 1932
(Ice Is Forming Moon)

Tulugaq Kagagi —

I have been writing a lot of pictures and stories and ways of the Spirit-led life to you. That is what I have been drawn to do. I am going to write some odd things now. I cannot explain much about these things that I will write in the following letters, but it seems right that I am to tell you. They are strange happenings and visions that have occurred a few times in my life. Maybe it is that you will experience similar things. Maybe not. These things do not make a person holy or special in any way. I cannot say why I have had these experiences. They gave me strength and hope and they encouraged me. How? I do not know because they are strange. These happenings were filled with a strong presence of the Everlasting One and my mind was filled with visions and my body with life.

So, I will tell you of these strange occurrences.

Here is number one ...Many snows ago I was taking a walk to another small waterway near our cabin. I asked to see the Creator more plainly. As I was getting close to the waterway, I became very much aware of the Spirit's presence in all things. It was like the trees and ferns and rocks were looking at me. Even the air was like a person, a being. It was clear that everything contained Spirit's presence and I was being observed by friendly and caring life all around. They were humored by my appearance and I began to laugh at them because they were no longer hiding from my eyes and I saw that all was smiling. I was seeing more clearly the essence of Spirit in all things, and joy and laughter came out of my heart. I was talking to the trees and the rocks, but they did not talk back. Yet, it was so natural to be talking to them. I was seeing the unity, the oneness and relationship of all in the Spirit. I was filled with amazement about the thread of Spirit that is operating on all levels. It was good.

Here is number two ...This happened long ago when I was at the church in Brochet. I stopped in there to visit the man who cleaned the building. His name was Frank. We were in town to sell skins and take dried fish to friends. Adik was visiting her cousin, so I went over to the church. Pembina stayed with Adik to play with his little friends. He was maybe ten snows. I went into the main building and it smelled very nice. They smoke the building with a tree resin from the lands near where Geezus was. Someone was playing a piano, so I sat down to listen. When I closed my eyes, I saw a most Beautiful Thing. Like a sphere, but not round. More like a wewe (goose) egg but the surface was covered with countless small areas like a mikinaak's (turtle) shell and they had all the colors on them that must exist. The colors were not so much on the surface as they were flowing out of the surface like water from inside. The colors were shinning like metal or glass shines in the sunlight. There were transparent beings, like smoke, moving around and around the Beautiful Thing. I was made aware that the Presence, the Eternal One was within the beauty. The Creator was this Fountain of Life and the Beautiful Thing was the way I was allowed to experience the wonder of the True Light of Life. I was overwhelmed with wonder. I cannot say it with words. It was good.

Here is number three ...When I was maybe fourteen snows old, it was before I went south, I sought a vision from Creator for my life path. I was fasting, and after a sweat lodge I went out by myself to see if I would be sent a vision to help lead me as I grew up. I made my questing place in a shallow depression about the size of our cabin. There were many large rough rocks in this hollow. As I waited there I was visited by two cranes and a fox. They were not afraid and studied me. I thanked them for bringing me their words. I did not hear them speak, but they spoke into my mind of our relation to each other.

After they left, a bird that is called by the whites, Rose Breasted Grosbeak, flew up to me and sat on a stick. This bird comes here only now and then because it is far north for them. The male bird is black with a red chest and white underside. But this one had something strange, he had one yellow feather in the center of his chest. This was a powerful sign. This bird was bringing me all the sacred colors of the four directions: red, yellow, black and white. He was naturally not made to carry all these colors but Creator gave him the one yellow feather to make him complete and to bring this message to me. I felt that Creator was confirming to me in this sign that all the world is being drawn together into one body. Like the bird with the four colors, all the peoples of all the directions, red, yellow, black and white, are now starting to be drawn together and after many more generations and lessons the people of the world will slowly come to acknowledge the unity of the one body of the one family. Each will be proud and cherish their uniqueness, but also honor all as sisters and brothers.

When the bird flew away, I turned my eyes to the many large rough rocks sitting before me and they all were possessing many different and ancient faces of the grandmothers and grandfathers. They became alive with their faces fixed on me, and though each one was different, they were all speaking the one Truth of the unconditional love and acceptance that is in the universe. I was filled with peace and amazed at the power of this understanding to drive away insecurity. I returned their gazes with my face of love and soon a large Kinew (eagle) with a great wingspan flew very close to my vision questing place. He was telling me that what I needed to receive at this time was done. My quest was over. It was good.

This is number four ...There was a day when I was singing my songs and praying when I saw four silver columns arranged in a square extending out of sight into the sky and out of sight far below. Their silver color was so pure that it was transparent. They were a symbol of perfection and the four columns seemed to sing out a tone of someone humming. It was like an eternally pure sound. Then from the distance came a vapor like Being at great speed. As it came, it left a trail of itself behind that slowly faded away. The vapor like Being flew around and inside the silver columns until it had wrapped them up with itself. That was end of this vision.

After many days it was revealed to me that the columns were me and that the God of the spirits, in grace and love, viewed me in my essence as good and pure. The sounds of my life path were a beautiful harmony and, like all people, the more I was aware of the Great Being wrapping around me the more the song of life would be heard by others. It was good.

This is number five ...Just after I took Adik to myself and she took me to herself, I was far down the lake in a jiimaan (boat) with my father and a storm came up. The cloud people were blowing furiously. We were too far to make it home. He and I had to head for land and the storm lasted for some days. It blew so long and hard that we set up a camp with a canvas and dragged the boat up on the rocks and turned it over for protection from the rain and cold. I got tired of sitting under the boat after a couple days. I took a walk along the shore that was all big boulders. The sky was low with gray and blue clouds. The wind was still driving high waves against the rocks. A long way down the beach a shaft of light caught my eye. It was a thin stream of light going down behind a dense growth of black spruce trees. I climbed up the shore and went through dead branches. There was a small clearing filled with mosses and blue berries and one iris that was blossoming. When I stepped into the clearing and into the narrow stream of light, I was filled with a great sense of wonder at the beauty of the spot. The cold left my body and warm contentment filled me. The impatience of having to sit for days left and my inner person was filled with ease and I was very peaceful. This came from outside and seemed to enter me through the light. There was also what seemed to be beautiful voices like many women singing in the distance that I could not understand. There were clouds moving through the sky, but the shaft of light seemed to divide the clouds when they came close and it kept shining. It was not normal for clouds to act like that. I was very much aware of being safe in a universe presided over with love and care. Maybe it was because I had been stuck under a boat for so long a time that my being was so happy to see the light. I do not know these things of the mind, but I do know that I was touched by a medicine like none other. A great love. The storm finally let up a little and we made it back to Brochet. Everyone was happy to see us. It was thought maybe we had overturned in the lake. As I pondered the days of the storm, I decided it was a good thing it came our way. If the storm had not come, I would not have been touched by the light. It was good.

I have written enough for now. These are mystical things. They are good things that may happen to us. They encourage and cause us to wonder and crave more of the Great Mystery. But, the best thing is a steady walk into growing to know the kindness of God. I will write more of these mystical things in the next letter.

Love,
Mishomis Minominike Gissis Makwa

Letter Thirty-Four
3—*Gashkadino Giizis* 1932
(*Ice Is Forming Moon*)

Tulugaq Kagagi —
Here are some more spiritual happenings and visions.

Number six ...This happened when I was singing and I was lifting my hands to the four directions. To Gichi Manidoo I was offering my thanks for being given my existence. Right away I saw myself standing in front of the One Who is the Beginning and the End. The Wonder of Forever was looking at me. I looked down and I saw that I was without any clothes on. I was naked. The Holy One was like a mother and father in one being. As I stood there, the Holy One was looking at me with pride and I heard these words in my heart ..."You are beautiful." This I understood to mean that in my openness and bareness I was looked upon as perfect in His sight. I knew that this was also how the Father-Mother Being sees all of the human family. It made me happy. It was good to hear this.

So, here is number seven ...This vision happened one night when I was sitting in my chair listening to the wind in the trees. It was a vision of a feather that floated down from the Rider of the Heavens. The feather hung in the air before my eyes. To this day I am always picking up feathers wherever I find them. I have a box filled with feathers of many kinds because I am drawn to them. I believe it was a vision of how the Spirit works in us. Gentle, but strong and with authority like a feather commanding the air it moves. Maybe I will take my feathers with me when I fly through the western door.

The feather in the vision was black, but I did not view it as blackness in which there is nothing visible to see. It was a perfect feather that was similar to feathers midway on the wing of a binayshee (bird). I could see every barb and every tiny part of each barb, even the hooks. All these and the quill and shaft were flawless. It was gentle and weightless, yet strong and commanding. The black contained hidden colors like you can see in the feathers of kagagi (raven) when turned in the sunlight.

This black feather, when I saw it in my vision and was experiencing its Power within my being, was filled with tenderness and authority. I think this feather is like the binayshee (bird) that is said came down and landed on Geezus when He was in the river. That feathered one was a picture of the Spirit coming on Him and creating in Him power and understanding of His mission. It was a sensitive and kind Spirit yet full of power and overwhelming. It is said He was driven and led by the Spirit into a wilderness area after that. This is what the feather seems to speak to me. It shows me the Spirit comes to us, rises up in us and gives direction. As the delicate feather of a bird gives power to fly, so, too, the Spirit gives us power and gently leads us or commands us inwardly to be driven along. This was a vision that I have often pondered upon. It was good.

This is number eight ...It happened during a season when I was not settled and I was anxious about many things. I could not seem to be at peace with myself and my mind was preoccupied with the business of life and responsibilities. I think it was when I was building our new cabin for Adik after we were married. Into my mind came these images of the Eternal One coming across the sky. There were many tall clouds, and down through these great billows of white clouds came the Ancient of Days as traveling surely to a destination. The Great Traveler had long hair that flowed behind. All around were messengers and beings traveling too. The Ancient One was covered with a heavy cloth of many folds. There was no design on this cloth. It was the color of the inside wood of the spruce tree under the bark. A living color. I was caught up into the cloth and held in the great folds as we traveled through the sky. I was held safe, close to side of the Timeless Traveler, and the cloth trailed out of sight far behind us into the unending heavens. I was not alone in these folds. As the cloth shifted in the wind, many different folds appeared with many beings caught up in them. There were relations of all kinds: black people, red and white people, people from Asia that I have seen in a book. There were animals from all over the world and birds, fish and bugs and plants. All life was being carried along.

As I came away from this vision, I realized that my life, the life of those in my world and the life of all things is being carried along by our Maker. We need not think that we are entirely responsible to make it all happen according to the way we think it should. Our Maker knows the destination, and we will lovingly and securely arrive there. We need not be so worried as we travel our life path. This put my head and heart back together so my life and responsibilities were not overtaking me.

I have other mystical things that have happened, but most I cannot put into words. They were given to me and maybe they do not speak so much to you. So, I will only tell you one more.

Here is the last one, nine ...This happened to me many snows past. I was young and strong, very strong and confident in myself. Too much so. I was in the town and there were many people gathered. I do not remember why so many people were there. Maybe it was for the spring shipment of things from the south, but there were a lot of people waiting on the shore. It was a long wait and someone started singing one of our songs about Kinew (eagle) flying up to God and lots of people were singing. Me, too. Suddenly I could not breathe very well. I started to breathe like a dog does after running. I became very weak and could not stand so I sat down on a stump. I was a little embarrassed. People gave me room, but they were not concerned and kept on singing. Soon I could not even hold my head up and a deep humility came over me as I was sensing Creator becoming very real with me. It was His presence that was bowing me down. There was an overwhelming majesty and I saw my arrogance and conceit for what it was. A selfishness that was not wholesome. As I sensed Creator's presence, I was staggered by the humbleness of the Most Powerful One, the Almighty One, the Everlasting One Who Stretched out the Earth. I was seeing that the love of my Maker for me was so great that He would give away all power and splendor, if that is what it took, in order for me to know Him. I saw clearly that this was the perfect picture of Father's Love that Geezus was showing us in His life and by His great giveaway of His life. I was brought low in my heart by this wonder. My strength and power was nothing before the Great Humility. I saw that this meekness was true authority, this gentleness was true power, this love was the greatest strength in all the creation and it would never fail. After a long time my strength returned and my breathing become normal. I raised my head and sat up on the stump. Most all the people had gone, but a friend named Thomas had stayed with me. I didn't know what to say. I had become undone, but it was a wonderful and good thing.

This is all I will write about some of the unusual spiritual happenings and visions I have had. These were special things to me. But, you must know that these things do not make a person special. Having a vision or a dream or a happening is not what makes a spiritual person. It is trust in the Love that is better. Why some things may happen that are peculiar I do not know. Maybe they are given to those who are weakest to encourage us. Whatever the reason, it is good to simply trust that there is security for us and to walk our life path knowing Gichi Manidoo is with us. Life is a continuous spiritual experience in which the Spirit is always being revealed all around us and in all people. Some see, some have a hard time seeing. We move in and out of this seeing. Do not be afraid to tell of experiences you have, but seek the permission first of the Vision Giver. It might be that your special happening is for another, too, and you're telling of it may speak to them.

So, Tulugaq Kagagi, the days are getting shorter and the ice is coming again. All the bugs have been gone for some time now and Makwa (bear) will soon be taking his sleep. You and James and Peepeelee were here a few days ago and said that Lawrence was also coming for a visit this moon and he will bring you along with him. Adik is making some sweets for your visit. You and Lawrence will be staying a couple days. It is good to talk, and Lawrence helps us, too. He will split some wood and cook with Adik. We will send treats back with him to take into town for Father Engolf.

Adik wishes to tell you something.
Now Adik is speaking.

. — . — .

Hello there little man. I am making you some treats with sugar that we got from the store. I am going to tell you something that will help you understand what I have seen of Gichi Manidoo. This is understanding that many miss seeing, but is true. When people think of Creator, most have a picture of a nini (man) in their head. It is true that when Gichi Manidoo came as a human to show us of the nature of the Great Mystery, it was a nini (man), Geezus, but Gichi Manidoo is ikway (woman), too. You can see this in the Geezus man. Geezus was a life giver, like a woman, he birthed life in people. He was tender and compassionate, like a woman, with those in need of care. He nurtured people as a woman nurtures her children. He fed people like women do their children and family. He gave His life as a woman gives her life to her family. The Creator's family is the whole world. All people have been born out of Creator like children are born from a woman. The manly and the womanly nature are both equal in Creator and make up the Complete Being. It is good for you to think on this and let Creator's womanly qualities speak to you. Woman and man aid each other to be whole and in balance. We are equal but not complete, and we are in need of each other. Think on these traits that are in balance in our Creator and you will understand better and be in more harmony as a person. This is why Lawrence and others like him are special, because he speaks to us of the unity of womanly and manly. I wanted to tell you of this because Mishomis Minominike often speaks of the Creator as a man when Creator is not a manly being nor a womanly being but is the Being from whom both man and woman came. The Master of Life is Unique Being. One-of-a-Kind Being. Not a man, not a woman, but both and neither. Isn't that odd and marvelous? I saw this revealed to me once in a spiritual vision of mine, too, and I thought because Minominike was writing about some of his experiences I would tell this. This may be a different thing for you, but I have seen this truth.

I love you,
Nokomis Adik

- — · — ·

I, Mishomis, am speaking again now. This was a good thing for Adik to say. I remember when she told me of this revelation she had in a vision. It was a confirming teaching for her and for me, too. She had wondered about it to herself for a long time, and her vision helped her to see the truth of this. Same is true for me when she told me. So, here is a good example of a person telling their spiritual experience and having it teach another, too.

Yes, the Creator is both and neither. Creator is a Holy One-of-a-kind Being of Perfection, Mother and Father, Parent of All.

Love,
Mishomis   Minominike   Gissis   Makwa
(Grandfather Rice Moon Bear)

Letter Thirty-Five
Manidoo Giizisoons 1932
(Little Spirit Moon)

Tulugaq Kagagi —
You are growing so fast. Happy birthday to
you. You were born in Gashkadino Giizis (Ice Is
Forming Moon). James and Peepeelee had a
birthday time gathering for you at their cabin a
few weeks ago. You are five snows old now. You
and I have been having many talks and I see the
strong voice of the Teacher Within speaking with
you. The Teacher is heard more easy when we are
young and voices of the world have not yet
become so loud. I gave you another carving for
your birthday time. You still have the two Kagagi
(ravens), the Kinoje (pike), the three spruce dogs
named Kaniq (Frost), Nanuk (Bear), and Dende
(Bullfrog), and the carved canoe I made for you
on your fourth birthday. You have not lost
anything yet. I made the canoe big so that all
the other toys ride in it. For your fifth birthday I
gave you a carving of me and Adik sitting side by
side. We are just the right size for fitting in your
little carved canoe.

Adik's heart has been paining her more. It is
hard for her to make the walk to your cabin. She
rests often along the way when she hurts. We have
lived with each other for 60 some snows now. We
know each other well. Peepeelee comes over a lot

to help and visit and you run along, too. Now the snow is building up and getting too deep, so you will be riding in a toboggan and your dog will pull you.

When I saw Father Engolf last time, he showed me a gift that was given him by a hunter from the south. It was a binocular. A long time ago I saw one of these while in Winnipeg at the school. I have never owned one. You look into them at things far away and the thing becomes close to you. When I was looking across the lake through Father Engolf's binocular, it was like I was looking into the future. Reindeer is not yet frozen, and when I was looking, the waves were coming immediately to me, but when I lowered the binocular it took time for waves to arrive at my spot.

This came to me. When I look across the waves of Reindeer Lake with the binocular of my spirit, it is like looking over the human family of the whole world. The energy of the Spirit wind is moving our hearts along to be filled with freedom and compassion instead of fear and domination. I see that the longing of every person is to experience inner peace and joy and live out a life of love.

I saw, by using the binocular, that if I look too close at the lake, all I see is confusion. All looks in chaos. When I raise the binocular to take in a bigger picture I see that the waves far out on Reindeer are being moved along by the single purpose of the Wind. When we focus too close there appears no direction and much turmoil in the world, but when we raise our gaze to catch the Wind's work, we can see its purposeful intention.

When I look into the future, how far I don't know, I believe I see people will come more and more to understanding the deception of the false voice that makes us insecure, fearful and self-protective. The Teacher Within speaks to the heart of all people to be aware of the lying voice, but the mind, where the false voice lives, keeps screaming out its lies. It is my sense that the binocular of my heart shows me the Spirit Wind will be having its way. I believe more and more will discover the liar and begin the renewing of their mind. Clouds will pass and the beauty of all things will be uncovered for many people. The world will begin to know we can live together in one room.

Here is something else I wish to say, I don't think I told you this before. You and I go walking in the woods a lot and our path is always going around things—like the animal trails. We, and they, cannot just walk straight because of trees, rocks and springs and other things. A crooked path is natural thing. So, too, is our life journey.

So don't worry about making these detours or even taking a wrong trail every now and then. That's the way things are.

A while ago you and I were out too late and ended up in the woods at night. So, we just looked up and found the Ahnung (star) we needed to bring us in our general direction. We ended up walking in places I didn't want to be in but we knew that the river would show up sometime. When it finally did we just followed it downstream to the cabin and were home. So, too, is our life. If you end up lost and confused because you weren't paying attention or got distracted, just find your Star to get your bearings. He is waiting to take you back in a direction so you get on the path again. These things happen to every person in the life, like in the woods.

It is snowing again. There is a lot of snow already this year. That is good. It has been dry, as I said in a letter awhile back. Some of the ponds are low and Reindeer is even lower than I remember. This snow can be piled up around the cabin too and keep us warmer.

Love,
Mishomis (Grandfather)

Chapter Fourteen: Holy Carelessness

I got up from the table where I was reading the letters and pulled out an old wooden box from the corner. Balancing on the box I peered over the edge of the loft toward where I had found the letters and bear hide. There they were, the carved toys from Minominike, none the worse for wear. Two ravens, three dogs, a pike, canoe and two older looking people in seated pose. They were just beyond reach. I jumped my midsection up onto the edge of the loft and held on with one hand while reaching far enough with the other to tow them closer.

Longing for the innocent and carefree days I had spent with these toys, a question came to mind. How is it that we lose the wonder and joy of our youthful freedom? Our imagination seems boundless, our curiosity never ending. As we grow up, the child within is hushed and pushed aside but steadfastly refuses to leave no matter how much we demand its silence. Our inner child stands in the shadows, eyes flashing with the fire of adventure and awe, waiting for release.

As I looked the toys over, imagining my play with these old friends, I was attracted to the eyes. Although this did not stand out from my childhood, it was obvious that Minominike had stained red the eyes of each toy. I recalled that red is the sacred color of life. I harbored the thought that in his wisdom, knowing the genius and necessity of play to bring vitality to our lives, he was investing sacred life onto each of his creations.

My inner child stepped from the shadows as I soared the two ravens above my head, swam the pike into the deep under the table and sent the dogs on each other in play. Minominike and Adik sat in the canoe and journeyed the full interior of our cabin, now transformed into lake and stream. It came to me that our approach to life must essentially be one of holy carelessness resting in the faith that all is ultimately well and will be covered with Love. This is the understanding that brings the sacred color of life to flash from our eyes.

Letters Thirty-Six through Forty-Three

Iskigamizige Giizis

Letter Thirty-Six
Iskigamizige Giizis 1933
(Maple Sugar Moon)

Tulugaq Kagagi —
It has been over four moons since the last letter. Your Grandmother Adik passed on through the western door a few days after I last wrote to you. There are tears when I remember her and will probably be tears until I leave, too. Over 60 snows we were together. She was a kind person to me and knew me well. She gave us three children, as I have said before. They all passed on before her and I believe they are in each other's presence now.

There was half-moon the night she left, and it was cold. We were in bed with the bright moon shining through the windows. Her chest and arm was hurting, but we were talking about the snoring being made by our old dog Willie with the two missing toes. Then, she wanted to talk about Albert and Angeni and Pembina. I was telling her about little Pembina and the first time he catch a kinoje (pike) and some namebini (suckers) at the mouth of the river and she was squeezing my hand tightly not letting up. I thought she was being loving, as she often did. When she finally let go, I hear her breathe out and then all was still. When I sit up to look at Adik, she had left me. Willie got up and came to the bed where he sat looking. I took Adik in my arms and said nothing. We stayed together in the bed that night, and next morning I put Adik's favorite clothes on her and wrapped her in the big Hudson Bay blanket we got from her mother a long time back. I left her hair unbraided. Old Willie watched all this from his place by the stove and didn't move. I put ahsayma (tobacco) in the blanket and cedar. Then, Willie and I cried and sat and told Adik how much we loved her and thanked her for all she gave to us and I said I was sorry for things I may have done that hurt her. I lay on the floor most of the day in sorrow.

When the moon came up again Willie and I set out to walk to your cabin and tell you and James and Peepeelee. You did not understand, but you knew we were sad. As we stood together, you hugged each of our legs to make us feel better. Maybe you will remember that night.

We walked back to my cabin late and started up the fire. My mind was not with me and I had forgotten to keep the fire going through the day and even left without stoking or banking it. Peepeelee, James and I cried again. You had fallen asleep in the toboggan that Kaniq, Nanuk, and Dende pulled along. Everyone went to sleep and I went out on the porch and watched the dancing spirit lights in the night sky. They were beautiful and moved so gracefully over the cabin from horizon to horizon. Even though the moon was up shining, the lights could be seen dancing and waving like big sheets, and there were even visible the sparkle of the brightest stars through them.

Next day I wanted to take Adik outside to her praying place by the river and where it was cool for her body. James and Peepeelee carried Adik in the beautiful blanket to her spot. We built her sacred fire there and I stayed with Adik and tended it. Many pleasing remembrances came back to me over next days as I stayed at the fire. There are so many, but I feel like sharing just a few with you.

I remember the first time I touched her. We were walking to the lake after I was eating supper with her family and, when we were behind a tall rock, I was drawn to reach out and touch her cheek. I was sort of standing behind her and my touch startled her. She stepped away and put her hand to the spot and was looking at me. When she smiled, I knew it was okay. I can still remember how her cheek felt that first time.

I remember when I first made her cry. I was tired and in a bad mood because I had a lot to do with building our cabin. Things were not going well with the building. She came to see me and bring some food but was later in getting there than I expected. We were sitting on part of the cabin wall and she saw that it was not level. When she looked at the logs in a puzzled way I yelled at her and said a curse in my frustration with the building. I walked away telling her to leave me alone. It was part of me that she had not seen and she was scared. I stood by the river and knew I was wrong in what I had done. When I came up the bank she was crying. We came to each other and she said she was sorry, but really it was me who did the offense.

When Albert was not yet born Adik was very sick. She was throwing up a lot. I remember thinking how much she gave herself in love to me to be willing to go through this. Even after a hard birthing time of Albert, she said that the joy of our relationship made her think of the pain as a small thing. She was happy to see me happy.

When my father was old he was getting forgetful and also bad tempered. He lived with Adik and me for a few months before he died. It was very hard for me because he was so irritable, but Adik said we had to see beyond this change in him, and love and care for him. I remember how much she ignored his criticisms and still was gentle and honoring of the person inside. She truly could see the beauty and dignity that he was in spite of the rough bark on the outside. I was amazed at her caring spirit. This never left her. She taught me much about the love of God.

Adik loved to give food to people. She was always cooking up something. Whenever people had a sickness or tragedy or a marriage or celebration of some kind, she wanted to bring them food. This was her way of giving of herself and saying she cared. Every day she would make me food with this love and she was the best at cooking. No man ever had food as good as I did.

This is a funny remembrance. One time Adik was angry at a dog we had named Chi Wajiwan (Big Mountain) because he pulled down some meat we had drying. She had worked so hard at slicing and preparing it. When she picked up the mess I could tell she was going to get that dog. As she carried the meat to the cabin the unruly dog got in front of her and she almost tripped over the beast. In her angry state, she kicked out at the fellow's rump and ended up breaking her toe. The dog took off without harm and hid under the porch. Now Adik was really mad. She wanted to beat that dog, but her toe was telling her to leave well enough alone because maybe something worse will happen. I wanted to laugh, but I knew if I did I might be next to get a kick in the rump with her other foot. She could tell I was holding back my smile and she made me go out and yell at Chi Wajiwan who stayed under the porch until darkness. When he came out, he kept his tail between his hind legs. I wrapped a couple of her toes together to help the broken one mend. Adik walked around like ziishiib (duck) with a bad foot for some time until she healed.

So, these were some memories. There are so many things that come back to me about our 60 some snows together. It went so fast. She was my girl with the large caribou eyes.

James started to build another fire not too far away from where I was sitting with Adik and taking care of her sacred fire. He did this to thaw the ground for her grave because it was still frozen. After a while we thought it better for her resting place to be near Angeni, Albert and Pembina and Onaiwah. He went into Brochet to Father Engolf and to thaw the ground there. Father Engolf and Lawrence came to sit and help tend her fire with me. They are such good friends. Four days after Adik passed on, we loaded the toboggan and went to Brochet. James had thawed the ground and dug her grave. We told Adik's spirit to leave and go on to Gichi Manidoo and we put Adik next to our children. We had a meal at Lawrence's house and gave thanks for the beautiful life that she lived.

I am now heading to bed. Willie has been sleeping next to the bed to keep me company. He knows of my loneliness and is heartbroken too.

Love,
Mishomis   Minominike   Gissis   Makwa
(Grandfather Rice Moon Bear)

Letter Thirty-Seven
1—Aabita Niibino Giizis 1933
(Halfway Through Summer Moon)

Tulugaq Kagagi —
Lawrence has been with me for a few days. He came out because he was told by Great Spirit I was lonely. A pair of kagagi came to his home and when he saw them together it came to his heart that I must be missing companionship because Adik is gone. The pair kept flying at him where he was splitting wood and so he put down the axe and came out. He brought some fancy expensive canned food from the store and bottles of ginger ale. The bubbles and his company are helping to lift my heart and make my face smile easier. Kagagi knew that it has been hard for me. They show us that we are never really alone, but still we can be lonely for our human companions.

Lawrence mentioned that he has met another man from Cranberry Portage and they enjoy each other's company. His name is Wapasha (Red Leaf) and he was born among the Dakota people far south in United States. This Wapasha might come live with Lawrence. I am happy for him.

I have not had much energy to write you lately. I am sorry for that. I think it is because of the hole in my heart that Adik's passing made. There are many thoughts of spiritual things racing through my head. Questions without words and the answers cannot be known in this life. It is for me to trust that even though what I do not understand is so much greater than what I seem to understand, all is held together by love in the arms of the Great Mystery. I suppose this is why the Ultimate Reality is called the Great Mystery. Our minds and our hearts are too small to get around this. When we come to times such as the passing of one so close, like my Adik or my children, we can do little but abandon ourselves to hope and let the Spirit speak away the sting of death. My inner man possesses the hope that just as our Being has inhabited this skin from the earth so, too, our Being wears a skin from the undying Spirit. This is spoken to me all around. All visible things change in time, but He Who Creates, the One Who indwells and empowers all forms of this visible world is timeless. The life giving Spirit that works in you and in me and makes all Beings and things is from everlasting to everlasting. Spirit is eternal because Spirit is beyond time. So, the loving power of the Spirit upholds our Beings when we leave behind this earth skin and journey into His Presence.

Lawrence called me for supper a while back but gave me time to finish the thoughts above. He has asked if I want the last ginger ale or if I want root beer. This meal will be good.

Love,

Mishomis Minominike Gissis Makwa

Letter Thirty-Eight
2 —Aabita Niibino Giizis 1933
(Halfway Through Summer Moon)

Tulugaq Kagagi -
I am writing right away again because Lawrence wants to speak to you. We finished the supper he made. He brought out tomatoes in a can and something that looked like a thin red tomato called a pepper and mixed them together with some rice and moose gravy. I had tomato in Winnipeg once, but never had these peppers. Very hot and spicy so you have to drink a lot. Lawrence experiments with food he gets at the store. He has store manager order special things just for him. Now Lawrence will write in his own hand.

- — · — ·-

Hello, my friend. I bet you never thought you'd hear from me in these letters. Your Mishomis told me you may not read this letter for some time, but I'll write some things in it to remind you of our current friendship. When I leave this old man's cabin tomorrow, I will stop in to your place and we'll swim in the lake. It's still quite cold for mid-summer, but it is always refreshing and good to feel clean. When we swim you hang on to my long hair and I tow you around. You laugh and we have a great time. Peepeelee brushes out the snarls you put in it when we're done. Your brown hair is like your first father's. I wonder what he would think if he saw how long his white son's hair has grown.

Sometimes I come out to visit and cook a special meal for your Mishomis. Next month my new friend Wapasha is coming from Cranberry Portage. I sent him word to bring along new foods that the store here does not have. Cranberry Portage is close to Flin Flon where the railroad is and they have several stores there.

My dog had three pups last week. Last time I was down visiting Wapasha he gave me this dog as a gift. He had named her Winona (First Daughter), which is a Dakota word. So, now I have four dogs! I'm sure some of the young people in town will adopt the pups. Winona is a basset hound and looks like a very large white and brown sausage. Needless to say I get a lot of smiles from the people in town when we walk around. There has never been a dog of this type here before and everyone loves her. Wapasha got Winona when he was in America last fall.

I think you are five-years-old now. I have known you since you were born and later adopted by James and Peepeelee. I made you a pillow as a gift for your bed on that bittersweet occasion. I sewed together many small pieces of beaver hide that I got from Mishomis and stuffed it with downy feathers from geese. I think it's your favorite thing in your big bed now because you always sleep with it even though you have a bigger pillow, too.

As you will remember, I like to cook. In a couple years, Peepeelee said you would be big enough to walk to my house in town and I will teach you some of my secrets about cooking. I purchased a cookbook with recipes from France when I was visiting Wapasha last time. It's been great fun but I often have to substitute certain ingredients that we do not have here in Brochet. I'm really looking forward to my next shipment of different food and spices.

Tomorrow I will help Mishomis with a fish trap in the river and then leave for your house. We'll clean the fish and he'll preserve them by smoking. He has a nice smoke house. The rabbits in there right now are almost done.

Your Mishomis finished washing the dishes while I was writing. We're going to sit out on the porch. I will smoke and watch the river while he writes some more. I'm glad to see him writing again. Adik's passing has of course caused him great loneliness. All of us miss her.

Your Friend   —   Lawrence   —Gi zah gin (I love you)

_._.__.

Hello, again. It did not matter to Lawrence if I read his letter to you so I will just write more on this paper.

Yes, I have a great loneliness inside, but I hold on to the hope I see in Geezus. He may have died, but came alive again. I have little understanding of His form after His new birth from out of death but people of that time could recognized Him. So, this brings me comfort when I think on the ones I loved that have passed on before me. I think we will know each other.

I am too tired to write more. I see by Lawrence's writing that you are going swimming with him. I should come along to watch the fun tomorrow. Maybe someday Gichi Manidoo will send a child Lawrence's way to take care of and raise-up. He would be a good parent and wouldn't get in the Master of Life's way when caring for a little one.

Love,
Mishomis Minominike Gissis Makwa

Letter Thirty-Nine
Manoominike Giizis 1933
(Rice Gathering Moon)

Tulugaq Kagagi -
Last moon, when Lawrence was here I walk with him back to James and Peepeelee's house where he was going to go swimming with you. That was a happy day. It was good for me to laugh and kid around again with the people I know.

On that day, you almost put that poor Lawrence under the water for good. You were hanging onto his hair from behind, as you do when swimming together, and he was towing you around. He got a cramp in his leg and at the same time in your playing you crawled up on his head. It was too much for him because of the big cramp from the cold water. It was deep in that spot and he went down but pushed himself off the bottom to get back up. He was coughing and reaching out to be sure you were safe and the dogs that were in the lake came over, too, because they sensed something wrong. It was a big commotion. James threw a long dry driftwood log out toward you and was taking his pants off to go help, but Lawrence caught the log floating by and made you hang onto it. You were coughing, too, and he was complaining with moaning from the cramp while he coughed. He chased the dogs away and made it to shore. It was a hilarious and fearful sight all in one. He was limping around rubbing his leg and hurting his feet on the stones and making strange noises and swatting horse flies that were attacking him. What a sight. We had a big laugh. Even Lawrence finally started to laugh. That powerful naked red man was gotten the best of by a little naked white boy and a few horse flies. I will never forget that. I asked Spirit to tell Adik about it. I know it will make her laugh too.

I had a bawazigaywin (dream) this last week that I am to tell you.

In dream I was walking in a large gitigan (garden) that I had seen a long time ago in the south. The dream garden was full of many different flowers and bushes and vegetables but it was not orderly like the one I had seen in Fort Garry. Fort Garry is now called Winnipeg. Similar plants were in bunches like they had been planted together, but everything seemed to have no order. The paths were hard to follow and I was having to struggle my way through all the different plants. I was picking berries and digging up ogeebiccoon (roots) and taking a handful of certain leaves to eat. Sometimes I would pick a flower and eat it too. Most what I eat would be hard to swallow, but once it was down it seemed good in my stomach and I thanked the plant. Some things I ate were to my liking right away. I found that I was in middle of the gitigan (garden) and confused about why was this gitigan so jumbled and chaotic? It seemed that the keeper of the gitigan didn't have a plan. All of a sudden the things I had eaten began to cause me to grow feathers like an owl and I started flying up from my spot in the gitigan. I circled higher until I could see the whole gitigan. When I got high enough, the meaningless chaos that it all seemed to be when I was in the middle of it started to have a purpose. I could tell that some bushes had to be planted where they were to give nearby flowers shade from the afternoon sun. Some plants were in a place for birds so they would guard a vegetable from insects. Everything was being worked for a good purpose by the keeper. When I was looking down through my owl eyes it all made sense and had a great pattern. I could see the keeper of the gitigan (garden) working in one of the areas to make everything purposeful. He was shaping, digging things and planting things.

There was a small wind blowing through the window when I came back from this dream. The wind seemed to bring these words to me — "Soon you will rise up and fly away to the One Who has loved you even before your beginning. Your gitigan is almost filled and the Keeper has been taking and planting and shaping the *happenings of your life for good beyond your understanding. When you fly to the Eternal One, then you will know just as you are known and you will see clearly and there will be no questions. The love, joy and peace that you have only tasted a little of will then fill you up."*

These words brought me contentment and tears came. After a while I went out to the river and I had a song and danced. Every time my feet took a step they were praying a thank you to the Dream Sender. I thought about my children and Adik and my friends that had gone on before me. And I wondered about those who would follow. All our gitigans are different, but each one is being taken care of by the Gitigan Keeper. Each one will be perfect even if they make little sense to us now.

It has been a while since the passing of the one who journeyed through this life with me. I feel that Adik is not too far from me. It is good to be coming back out of the twilight.

Remember the deep black spring about a day's walk to the north that my fathers would go to and that I went to when my children passed? I have gone there many times for many reasons. It is a sacred place for me. Someday James will show you the way to it. I am feeling that I should journey there again.

Be at peace little one.

Love,
Mishomis Minominike

Letter Forty
1 —Binaakwii Giizis 1933
(Falling Leaves Moon)

Tulugaq Kagagi -
I spent many days away from my home since I wrote last. These days were at your house with you and Peepeelee for a week while James was out with a hunter from the south. His name was Walter. When James came back, he needed my help. I went into Brochet with him and also got Lawrence and Father Engolf to lend a hand in putting up part of a big moose for winter. James was second time a guide for this hunter from the south and the man only wanted antlers. This was most beautiful moose I ever see to give himself away. We all shared his body. James kept his hide and I salted a lot of my part of the meat, and then they helped me bring my portion home to smoke.

After I got smoking done and cached away, I went off to the deep sacred black spring of my fathers. I was there four days. I felt the warm love of our Creator many times while there. I always take the canvas off the little lodge next to the spring and store it away, but I leave the framework. I had to fix the lodge this time because it was pulled down. I think a large animal tangled with it. I must tell James to show you the location of this place when you are older so you won't forget. It is given to my family by Creator as a healing place for our Beings and where we can meet with Him easier. You know that our Brother and Great Friend and Father is with us wherever and whenever we need Him, but sometimes it is easier for us to know this if we have a special place like this spring. Journeying to this place can help our hearts to hear Him within and around us. You can make a personal place of your own, if you want someday, and you can have this family place, too. It is for you to decide.

I took along my bundle of spiritual things I told you about in a letter, and after I repaired the lodge and put the canvas on and started my fire, I gave thanks and ate my last small meal for next four days. I smudged my body and sacred things with smoke and put out ahsayma (tobacco). I wanted to think only on the Great Lover and on my Adik and family and pray for His world.

You remember the letter I wrote about my time at the spring after Albert and Angeni pass on? Remember there was a black makwa (bear) that sat across from me in the fog and helped me to heal? Well, Makwa came again and sat across the spring. He startled me. I do not know if this was the same fellow because he would be very, very old, but maybe the Ancient of Days gave this makwa special grace to live this long and to come to me again. I would like to believe this. There he was sitting in the same place very soon after I entered my lodge. He must have been close by all along. When I sat looking out the door, our eyes met. The language of the Spirit is often spoken through the eyes. There was peace coming from him. No intentions of harm, only care for me.

My heart settled down from being startled and after a time of us looking at each other, gratefulness welled up inside me to be honored and visited like this again. My mind thought of the many good relationships I have been given. I thought of my grandparents, uncles and aunts and father and mother, brother and sister and many friends long since gone on. Of course I thought of you, my newest relation, and all these memories were like sweet blueberries and raspberries in my mind. I have been so blessed and I felt like maybe I wanted to pass on to be with the spirits of my past friends and wait there for all the world's family. Sharing love and having relationships is our most treasured thing to have in life. This is all we can truly possess and take with us. However, as I sat there I thought how much I loved the beautiful earth too and so I told myself I would stay a bit longer.

Let me tell you something I often do in helping my inner-self to have peace and know the Love. When I go to a place where there are people, I like to be still and watch them. I make believe that I am looking at them through the eyes of Creator Father. It never fails that soon my true Being rises up in compassion for each unique person I am looking at. Everyone becomes known for the beautiful and valuable brother or sister that they are. It is like I am seeing deeply. Maybe like Geezus saw all people. There is no bad judgment, only kindness, concern and oneness and wishing for them to also know their relationship and value in the eyes of Father God.

Through these eyes of the Spirit I am made aware that what I see is their real Being. In the next life these true eyes will be all that every person looks through. All in the family of man have these eyes right now and it is relationship with our Creator that reveals this to us. You can do this too. You can see the world through the eyes of the Spirit because His eyes are within you. Make a habit to do this and the truth of everyone's beauty can become part of your every day. Learning to see through the eyes of Truth is a privilege we have been given. However, I must confess that my natural eyes through which I usually look out at the world are quite blind.

So, after some time, Makwa got up and stepped to the spring. He bent down and drank and the ripples of his drinking came across to me. He was calling me to drink and I crawled ahead on my knees to the edge and put my mouth into the water. It was a good drink and the coldness was felt all the way down in my omisud (stomach). I can still taste it. The water dripped off my chin and my ripples mixed with his in the spring. We were both seeing into the dark water that was clear like the air in the night sky. Never did water bring me such goodness as this spring. Like many years ago, it was again like drinking in the life of forever.

As I was bent down, I could see a reflection of movement in the pool. I looked up and Makwa was standing on his hind legs across the spring. He was very tall and black like the deep water. He made no fuss and dropped to his front feet without a sound, but his weight made more ripples in the pool. The big fellow turned his back and disappeared into the tamaracks, making no noise. Where he came from and where he went is his knowing only. He was like the wind of the Spirit. It silently appears and you experience its presence and see its affects, but it is a mystery in its moving. I am glad the Spirit willed to come to me that first day at our sacred spring.

I slept well that night in the lodge. Early next morning there was frost on the grasses around the area and sky was colored like the little violet in the woods. There were visitors that morning, a pair of zhongwysh (mink), and a gawg (porcupine), many little feathered ones and, in the night, I heard a Bizhiw (lynx) in the distance.

I spent the days resting and praying and listening and seeing the hand of Gichi Manidoo in all that was there. I took the pipe often, smoked it sending out my prayers, and over the days, I continued to see the faces and remember many things of the people I knew. Again, there was a yearning to be going on, to be with each one that had already walked out their lives, but also there was a cord, like sinew, that held me here to be with you and James and Peepeelee and that old dog, Willie, and all the others. So, it is clear from my writing that I have not passed on and that the cord was stronger. It is not yet time.

I did not know how long I would spend at the spring, but on the night before the fourth day it felt like time to eat and make ready to leave this place. I put the canvas away and rolled up my bundle. I stood on the edge of the pool and looked again into its deep. A thought came to me that this was like the black western door through which we pass at death. It may look dark to us, but that is only because it has been catching and storing up all the light of our lives. Even the sun walks into it and seems to be gone, but that is only in our mind. The Light is there, just beyond the door.

My Being was caught up in staring into this deep. Then the star points of light in the night sky began to appear brighter and brighter in the pool until the water was full of these sky people. It was as if there was a heaven above and a heaven below. All things were seen as being united and I was in the center of His creation. My heart heard the Teacher Within say that each person living or who had ever lived or will live is always the center of His creation.

Some time passed and as the air was cooling, a vapor began to rise from the spring. Soon there was a tall cloud of fog like a spruce tree climbing high into the sky. This fog took on the light of the pool and sky. It looked like it was going up into the heaven and down into the spring. There was no dividing the below from the above.

After some time of watching this wonderful thing the cloud of light began to change. It became red and yellow and violet as the Great Light was rising in the east to circle the sky. Even though I could no longer see the stars, they were there wrapped up in the Great Light.

That night was a thing of wonder more than my ability to know.

Love,
Mishomis (Grandfather)

Letter Forty-One
2 —Binaakwii Giizis 1933
(Falling Leaves Moon)

Tulugaq Kagagi -
All the leaves are falling. A couple mornings
ago, I was falling, too. I slipped on the porch
because of frost. My head hit the chair out there
and I was carrying a bucket that my chest hit. I
broke the bucket and maybe a rib. My head is
fine. Just a swelling, but it is hurting to have a
big breath like a yawn.

I had a dream about Adik last night. She was
sewing a new patch on my canvas coat. I wear
out the elbows. That is all I remember. This
dream has made me lonesome for Peepeelee, so I
will come to visit you today. Maybe I will bring
my socks for her to darn up the holes. I can darn,
but it is not a thing I like to do.

Old Willie seems up for a walk, too. He is not
too stiff today. I am sure he would like to growl
at Dende, Nanuk and Kaniq and make his hair
stand up on his back. He thinks he's still a tough
fellow.

I have found a nice piece of spruce and will be
carving you another gift for your sixth birthday.
It is coming soon. I am going to carve an
airplane. These machines have been coming to

Brochet for some years now. I have never been in one, but I have seen them tied up to the dock in town. A couple times I stayed to see them fly away. They make a powerful noise and their engine blows the water into the air behind them when they leave. It is amazing that big machine can ride on the air. They are not as graceful as birds. When Adik and I first heard the noise of their engines coming from the sky and saw one flying it was a puzzling thing. We left our cabin and came into town to see it.

I will carve the toy in five parts and piece it together. The plane, the wing and the two floats and the propeller. This will take some time, so I am starting soon.

I would like to see the world from up in the sky. Someday you will ride in one and look out over the earth. Father Engolf has been up in one and Lawrence went to Flin Flon once. Lawrence said that he got a little sick because of the up and down in the wind when he was coming back. Still, it is something he wants to do again.

James is making you a small toboggan that is just the right size for you to drive with one of your dogs. When the snow comes this winter you will start learning how to drive it and control the dogs. Peepeelee said you are ready to learn. You are getting strong enough to use a sled. She said that when she was your age, her father taught her. I think it was easier for her to learn because James said there are no trees and only short brush where she is from. You will have to start on the lake ice where it will be open. One dog will be plenty for you.

I will be at your cabin before the sun goes down.

Love,
Minominike Gissis Makwa

Letter Forty-Two
Gichi Manidoo Giizis 1934
(Great Spirit Moon)

Tulugaq Kagagi -
It is now the short days and we are in a deep cold time of the beboong (winter). I have a good fire going in the stove and Willie is sleeping near it like he does. James piled plenty of wood close to the door so it can be gotten too easy. There is a great quiet over all the land. Sometimes a black spruce or poplar will send out a sharp crack in the stillness because the cold makes it split. There is frost in the cabin by the door and windows tonight. I always think about our relations the animals and how they survive these cold times. Maybe some do not.

It is a good night for listening to the whispers of God. I sense the timeless Spirit all around and it is as if my life is like the breath that floated from me when I went outside to get firewood. It was a beautiful vapor that hung in the air. A delicate and one-of-a-kind mist being taken back into the heavens that gave it. I thought these things while holding the firewood and standing in the light of the door watching my breath move into the sky.

Just like there are no two similar breaths formed in the air on nights like this, so, too, every

Being that is breathed into the world is shaped in a unique and beautiful way. Tulugaq Kagagi is a breath from heaven. You may often wonder what is the intent or purpose of your life. Like a vapor it may not seem to have a direction or purposeful shape. But the One who breathed you into Being takes all that is your privilege to experience, that which seems to you wasteful and bad and that which seems good, and shapes your Being into beauty.

I am going to write my prayer on this night.
- ———— -

Creator, you have put this in my heart for Tulugaq Kagagi. It is for all people, but I am thinking on him at this time. You have made it plain that the whole family in the earth and the heavens is to be called by Your name. We are sons and daughters of Gichi Manidoo. I desire, and I know it is Your desire, too, that the inner person of this little one be filled to running over with the life of Your Spirit. Also, I pray that he know you as Friend and Father like the Geezus man of long ago. He was called Son of God and we all are Your sons and daughters, too. It is my prayer that Tulugaq Kagagi knows he is buried deep in Love and can never be moved. Give him a trusting when he needs it so he knows that whatever he goes through in life you will take these things and turn them all for the good and the beautiful. You can and are doing wonderful things beyond what I can imagine or think and someday he, too, will come to know the name of his Being is same as mine, Inabiwin Pindig— Inabiwin Awass Wedi (Looks Within — Looks Beyond). Good night, Creator.

Love,
Minominike Gissis Makwa

Letter Forty-Three
Iskigamizige Giizis 1934
(Maple Sugar Moon)

Tulugaq Kagagi -

The Teacher Within is beginning to tell me that I have little more to say to you in these letters. The Spirit is saying that now these things are for you to learn. What has been said is enough. So, I will tie this letter with two cords of sinew. It is a cord that binds together the bodies of the living. One cord I make green for the earth and one blue for the heavens. This cord is our binding even after I am gone.

I have written much, but in all these words there has been really only one great Word. The purpose of each letter from beginning to end was summed up with the word "Love" and then I signed my name. It is this way with the letter of life. The beginning through the ending is written within "Love."

It is out of 'Love' that we come into Being. It is in the 'Love' that we pen each word in our letter of life, whether we know it at the time or not. It is to the 'Love' that we pass. Everyone's letter is his or her own story written on this paper of 'Love' and each letter is a treasure in the Book of Life. This is all that I have written. It is now for you to discover this Truth and to know your freedom in the love embrace of the universe.

We have many experiences and we chase after many things and there are lots of distractions that make us think we are hidden from the 'Love', but the presence of 'Love' is without limit and encloses us.

I am thankful that I have been allowed to write what I have, but I may not write anymore. I will soon be 82, or maybe it is 83 snows. I am being called back to be with the Father and Master of Life. It is soon that I think He is finished making me as He wished. In the life to which I go, I believe the boundary of my sight, my hearing, my knowing, my experiencing will be lifted. I will cross the frontier to know as I am known. The One and Great Knower will carry me on the eternal journey of unbounded living joy. I will commune with all my relations and with all the people of all time will I have friendship. I will sing and dance with the spirits of all beings.

I think I will walk to our sacred spring. Maybe I will meet with the Great Being and stay with Him forever.

Zahgidiwin (Love) is all there is.

Love,

Mishomis (Grandfather)

Chapter Fifteen: New World

As I finished the final bundle of letters, there at the bottom of the box lay a lone letter and a paper folded up like a pouch. The pouch contained tobacco as an offering. This final letter was not held together by a red string but with two fine sinew cords. One died green and the other blue, the colors of earth and sky. This letter was his good-bye. His handwriting appeared unsteady as if trembling, different than the others. He knew the end of his days in this world had come and the letter hinted an answer as to why I could never remember seeing his body.

It had been two days since reading the letters. Two days spent listening to the Teacher within thinking, reminiscing, praying. I stepped out onto the porch of our cabin into the silence of the morning air and face to face with a cloud of black flies. Had I been in my usual preoccupied state of mind, loathing and a dismissing motion of my hands would have been aimed their way. This day was different. They received instead, a smile, an acceptance and a knowing that these, too, were part of the beauty and wonder of Creator's work. Who was I to determine value and purpose? The words of Minominike, the power of the story of universal good news had released the vitality of my inner being.

My attention turned to our path leading to the stones along the shoreline of Reindeer Lake. I recalled a particular letter of Minominike's and, in my mind's eye, saw myself without clothes running to the lake with my dog, Dende. I was maybe five-years-old, free and taking in the Breath of Life. Involuntarily my eyes teared over as I inhaled this breath again. The Friend I had known, my Beloved, had never left. Tulugaq Kagagi had never been alone. The flies swirled and celebrated existence in their chaotic dancing, delightfully performing for the pleasure of God. Lightness, freedom, divine life, the Zoë of God was all around and had always been at hand.

The stones really were crying out in wonder and praise, even through the long years of my distraction. I had been struggling for the unnecessary approval and acceptance of God when it had always been there. It was in fact never an issue except in my own foolish, desperate and distracted mind. Such had been the condition most of my life. I had lived in grayness and sought fulfillment through the esteem of men, the attainment of knowledge and through amusement. For many years His still small voice had been given no regard as the deception of false securities presented themselves.

But this day! A new day! A new world! The reality of unending, immeasurable, transcending Love in all things. Embracing all things. Streaming from all things. The invisible Presence, untouchable but more real than my own self! This was beauty and truth. This day, the only now, was always at hand, hidden in plain sight. My mind, quickened from its dazed stupor, could see, hear, smell, touch and taste the jubilation of the universe, the revelation of the Spirit-that-moves-in-all-things, the divine creation within which our inner being dwells.

Walking the path to the lakeshore I inhaled deeply of the Breath of the Life surrounding me. Kneeling down, I touched the waters that had taken my first parents lives that spring day in 1928. I had been too young when they were taken to feel or know relationship with them. As the waters of Reindeer closed around my hands I was aware of their beings. Now, forty-four years later, I sensed my connection and I knew their peace, their touch, their communion with James, Peepeelee, Adik, Mishomis Minominike and the Ininiwok and all relations in my life.

Sitting on the stones, drinking in the unity and joy, I caught the shadow of a raven in the corner of my eye. Soon another and another arrived until the trees, roof of our cabin and the shoreline were filled with upwards of fifty of my namesake. A murmur of throat noises, soft cackles and bill clicks filled the quiet morning air. A single bird sailed down and for a short time balanced on the tangled driftwood root system that had beached itself on the shoreline long before I had been born. Out of her beak she dropped a small black feather the length of a finger and returned to her perch. Straight away, with a commanding racket, the entire gathering was airborne. In a whirlpool of clamor they circled over the cabin and my station on the lakeshore. Single file they started off to the east and the Cochrane River. Two birds remained dive-bombing my position. I picked up the feather I had been gifted and rushed to follow them down the old abandoned footpath. I really had no idea what I was doing, but I was filled with a curious energy to follow these coal-colored friends. Except for the two dive-bombers the crowd had long left me behind. As my chase slowed to a fast walk the pair kept just ahead, flying from spruce to spruce. I knew where the path led.

The roof of Grandfather's cabin was sunken down but the walls stood intact. My two black guides had silently parked themselves on the glacial stone chimney. Slowly opening the door I saw the remains of the bed Adik and Minominike slept in. I could see old Willie with his missing toes sleeping near the now rusted stove. The table was bearing the weight of the ridgepole and its sagging roof. Next to the door was the water barrel and I recalled Grandfather's letter about his dream of being trapped in a barrel. I backed out the door and walked around the side. The cache had collapsed into a heap and poplars were growing through its debris. All things return to mother earth, I thought.

As I turned toward the river and walked under my two friends on the chimney they began to banter. One reached with its beak toward the other and snatched out a small feather similar to the one that had been dropped for me near the driftwood. It glided down alongside the chimney and I picked it up. They blurted out a rasp-like call and headed downstream. The two small feathers I now held in my hand were a symbol. "Never alone," said Raven.

The river flowed as I remembered. I walked along the bank to the place where the bear tumbled into the water and where Adik and I would pick berries. As I came closer to the lake and the sand bar, I began to recollect Father Engolf watching the moose being tormented by the ravens as they dropped sticks on her back. I spoke a thank you toward the sky as gratitude to the ravens for leading me back.

Closer to the lake I came to the place where I imagined Adik and Minominike's son, James' father Pembina, had nearly drowned. Here he had learned to be free from struggle and rest in the stream of the love of God. I wondered about his stature and appearance and imagined him to be somewhat like Minominike.

Upon returning to our cabin I carefully laid the two gifts from the ravens alongside the downy goose feather in the quill box Adik had made for me. I then retrieved and unrolled the sacred bundle, the old and balding black bear hide that had once belonged to Grandfather. For all those years, James had preserved it for me in the loft under the box of letters. I searched out the letter that described the personal ritual Grandfather used to settle his mind in order for him to more easily commune with Spirit. Following his ceremonial description, I began to resurrect the ways of this man in my life.

The next morning, after gathering together a few of James' things in a pack, I headed toward Brochet. Most of my father's clothes I donated to the church, but kept a number of shirts. His smell lingered in the cloth and I couldn't part with them. I had collected sprigs of cedar leaves from around Grandfather's cabin and our home to put on the graves of Adik, James and Peepeelee. I searched for Albert, Angeni and Pembina and although they had to be near, the current pastor did not know of the location since many of the old wooden markers had returned to the earth along with the loved ones they watched over. Strolling around the cemetery, I found the graves of Lawrence and his friend Wapasha who had moved to Brochet to live with him. Such a kind man and friend he had been to my family. I thought about our reunion someday when I, too, would pass from this life.

During my time in Brochet, the Spirit of God remained strong. I felt that time, past, present and future, had condensed into the single wonderful now and all the people who had gone before were joined in a celebration of the Eternal Life. I sensed in my heart that I heard them saying with one voice — "all is joined in goodness."

Chapter Sixteen: Harmony of Heart and Mind

I spent several more days at our cabin and read the letters again and again, each reading warming anew the peace in my heart. I knew now what Mishomis Minominike meant concerning the difference between the Word of the Spirit and the words of the world that fill our minds. Somehow I knew the Spirit of God, the Teacher within, was speaking the ultimate truth of our unity, goodness and oneness within a universe created by Love. This was the kingdom of God. Though my state of enlightenment would ebb and flow, I had and was experiencing the security and divine life of this truth. Yet, the words of the world, ingrained in my mind, spoke conflict.

The path I desired to follow was this path of Truth, the Spirit of Life. Thinking of my life in the south, I questioned what I was to make of that history? Could this Life gracefully continue flowing within and around me or would it diminish over time? How had deception so cleverly grown and pushed aside the Spirit? How was I to rework the knowledge, the indoctrination of my schooling? What should I make of the years I embraced that which all along had been built on a false premise? How could so many, how could I for so long, have missed it? Was it possible to be reconciled with the false belief systems that divide humankind? Their view of a hostile universe and an angry God, I knew clearly to be a lie. How many "sins" do our fears and insecurities bring into the world because of this delusion? What would I do with the truth that enemies were simply a creation of our own ego's self-defense? What could happen within the family of man if the mind were relieved of this self-perpetuating fear? To what degree had I been an ignorant participant in the advancement and teaching of this deception? How entrenched was this lie within the institutions of religion, politics and economic systems? Was there hope for change? Could the sleeping world be revived to the reality of 'kingdom of heaven within our midst', 'near', 'at hand', 'within you' as Jesus had said? What would be necessary, if anything, to live this out in daily life? Were all these questions distractions themselves that would hinder the profound truth of His Presence?

Reality had dawned in my heart. There was no turning back from this reawakening. The Great Mystery, the Lover of All Things was not distant. There was no need for shame, guilt, condemnation or blame. There is no liability for our humanity. This truth can release responsibility for change. Within the now of unconditional love, the sacred meaning of the name Inabiwin Pindig—Inabiwin Awass Wedi (Looks Within — Looks Beyond) was beginning to be understood. In his letter he had said this name, given to Minominike by Great Spirit, would also be given to me. Looking within to the Source of our being allows us to look beyond ourselves to the oneness of the relation we are with all things. Fear vanishes. Love becomes all and in all. Life, as intended, wells up and overflows. I was uneasy about returning to my old surroundings.

Chapter Seventeen: Deception

My days had been filled with nostalgia. I talked out loud to the dogs of my youth long since gone. I would take with me the old toys Minominike had made and a couple dozen old marbles rediscovered in the table drawer. Lawrence had picked them up in a store in Winnipeg and given them to me one Christmas. I thought about taking Peepeelee's ash basket of thread, needles, thimbles and patches that sat on the shelf, but I left it. The basket had probably not been moved since she died when I was 14. The cabin would be left pretty much as it was, for I would be returning.

I flew south in an old nine cylinder De Havilland Beaver with the co-op store manager and returned to the responsibilities of a religious career. I no longer felt a sense of urgency to bring people into subjection to a set of rules, dogmas and doctrines in order to satisfy a God seething with apocalyptic rage toward humanity. Quiet visions of Reindeer Lake, the uncountable stones of the shore, the ravens, meals of beans, fish and blueberries, my father and mother, our old leaky jiimaan were a continuing pleasure in my mind. The box of Minominike's letters and his bundle, along with the toys, occupied a shelf along the wall in my office.

During meetings with authorities and lay leaders of my religious denomination, now ridiculously trivial to my awakened heart, I sat amazed at the degree with which fear and its need to control, directed our decisions. Control, I knew, is not necessary when resting in the freedom of love's security. I had been freed from the compulsory need to govern and direct lives in order to keep them in the good graces of Creator.

I shared my reawakened understanding in conversations with friends. I told them that institution and ceremony can provide a sense of belonging, tradition and positive structures for life, but it can also enslave. If religion begins to limit relationships and divide the human family, or impose fear and separation between God and humankind, it has become evil. Laws, rules, regulations, dogmas and doctrines can rise to suppress the Spirit of Life. Depending on one's success or failure with walking the straight-and-narrow, a person might be guilt laden by failures or self-righteous with accomplishments. Either way we participate in determining self-worth instead of resting in His acceptance. My homilies declared the reality that laws, rules and regulations are not intended as ends in themselves. If they become such, they blind the vision of our spirit and no longer point away from themselves toward God. They obstruct the ever-fresh voice of God and imprison the heart.

I began to teach that religion can be a force for good. It can give us identity and roots and it can be a center for community. However, if religion creates 'the other', 'the outsider', or negates inner freedom, it has become destructive. Insights or ideas that originate outside the worldview of the religion, that do not fit within established doctrines and dogmas, find 'no-room-at-the-inn'. It is this inclination to promote division from the outsider, suspicion of the other and bondage to exclusive religious framework that veils our unity and oneness in the family of man, with God and with creation. They don't have to be, but religion and spirituality are often at odds.

Religion must promote the freedom of spirituality or it is a detriment to humanity's advance. Where the Spirit is, there is freedom. The more I spoke of this truth the more furrowed the brows of superiors and congregation. This was unfamiliar territory and unsettling to my parishioners who all their lives had known the false security of "coloring between the lines."

I told my church family of the one great truth — 'God is Love'— and love is not interested in control. The fruit of His Spirit is love, joy, peace, patience, kindness, generosity, loyalty, gentleness and self-control. If the Spirit of God gives us the gift of self-control, where did the idea come from that God seeks control of our lives? My congregation was fearful of freedom. The Spirit I knew desired only our freedom. Perfect Love drives away all fear and it became clear to me, where there is the need to control, fear subtly rules. If fear resides then the taste of perfect Love is not being experienced. If fear resides then perfect Love stands in the shadows.

Even though I knew there was disapproval within my congregation and from superiors I began to speak and write all the more of Creator's universal embrace. History shows us the results of the deception of exclusivist thinking. But history is not a reflection of ultimate reality, it is a reflection of the deception.

The day came when I felt the strong arm of the institution. Gerald, one of my superiors and a friend, asked to meet and personally explain the concerns of church hierarchy. I could sense his hesitancy at using his authority to muffle what he clearly saw had given me energy and life and might also do the same for others. We sat next to each other at his kitchen table enjoying rolls and hot chocolate while he explained that the traditions, position and power of the church were being undermined. He voluntarily admitted that the need to maintain hierarchical control and doctrine was at the root of my censor. He knew I would not be able to silence my spirit and in his heart-felt way told me that resignation would be better than removal. I knew there was no room for discussion within these iron walls. The idea and experience of a free and universal love was not possible because straying from the 'faith' and upsetting a god who kept score had eternal consequences. The costs, it was thought, were too high. The grip of fear was powerful and fierce. Gerald was hurt by what he was required to tell me and his moist eyes betrayed his care. There was no changing the minds of those at the top. We became even closer friends that day, but both knew sooner than later we would not share the same career. The hot chocolate gone, we walked a few blocks to a familiar café. Eating our salads, it was clear Gerald was returning to the contemplative man I knew. As I drank the cold water in my glass it reminded me of the waters of Reindeer. Someday, maybe not too far off, I would be drinking them again.

What I now understood was that at the foundation of individual egos reside fear and insecurity, and institutions, more often than not, are established and maintained for ego's sake. The ego justifies its primal fear through institutional approval. Extend this fear, individually and corporately, and it creates the ultimate fear, an angry god.

Exclusivist religion is birthed out of and dependent on an angry deity to cement and propagate its views in the consciousness of its followers and potential converts. It also invents a proper formula for appeasement of its god's anger. Those who 'believe in', accept and practice the 'faith' and become part of the chosen and exclusive group are smiled upon by their god. The ego is protected, reinforced and feels in control. Fear and insecurity is muted but remains the motivation for relationship with the god of the religion. A god created in the image of its followers.

I struggled with what seemed my impossible desire to remove the deception, to raise the consciousness of the institution I loved and had given so much of my life. The codified doctrines, laws written in stone, could not be questioned. I struggled in the tension that love and fear cannot coexist. The underlying grip of fear of displeasing God makes an enemy of the Father of Creation, an enemy of the Great Lover. This could not be further from reality! The fearful god of my institution threatened His creation with banishment, punishment or even eternal torment in order to inspire devotion and relationship. Thus a relationship of freely given love between created and creator was based on coercion, not choice. Here was the glaring contradiction within the cosmology of my training. God loves us, I was taught, but this god will torment us forever unless we love it back.

The lavish unlimited love of the Great Mystery, Minominike so clearly had relationship with, demanded nothing of His creation. I, too, knew this love and it was not coercive. The Spirit holds the world together by this Love. All creation, all humanity is connected, unified as one by the universal Spirit. Regardless of our delusion and error or the exclusivity of our claims to rightness and truth, the Wonder of Love has only one family.

I could not help but continue to point out the inconsistency of this fearful god. As I did so, the greater were the restrictions imposed by the authority of the institution. I was forbidden to communicate the radical, unconditional and ever-present Love being poured out on all humanity regardless of belief, acceptance or behavior. It was made clear—there were requirements on humanity. He demands our faithfulness. There are duties. There are obligations to be met in order to receive grace.

Obligations, requirements, demands, duties, faithfulness! Just what degree of holiness and sacrifice was enough to gain approval? Taken to its logical extension there was no end to the burden and liabilities. Jesus had invited humanity to lay down its burden and delusions of liability. Clearly the life-stealing and onerous burdens of law-based religion could never be met. The nagging of a law-based religious mind, struggling to meet its own internal demands, often creates a subtle paranoia and enslavement to chronic anxiety, fear and the delusion of God's displeasure because we can never measure up. Where, in law-based religion, was the free flow of peace and contentment in Divinity's Presence? Where was the rest in the arms of the Ultimate Love? Within a religion of demanding obligations, a person cannot know the freedom of the experiment of our lives. Minominike, although struggling and experiencing life's pains and questions as any human, appeared to, by-and-large, exemplify this state of freedom and of a being, living and walking in Love. And I, Tulugaq Kagagi, had tasted again the reality of the Universal Benevolence. Whether from an elitist institution or from one's own internal mental conditioning, the imposition of laws, rules and regulations boxes in the Great Spirit's expressions and can erase them entirely.

The mentality of gaining acceptance through behavior and belief naturally spawns a spiritual caste system. Spiritual experience and behavior is not a measure of our spiritual being. To gauge one's spirituality by number or degrees of spiritual experience or righteous behavior can be likened to determining the significance of a human being by race, sex or age. It is simply irrelevant. There is universal equality in the value of all humanity regardless of race, sex or age. We exist as triune beings. Created as physical, mental and spiritual entities. We are expressions of the Great Mystery. We are no more or less spiritual from other human beings than we are more or less mental or physical from other human beings. We are of one image. All human beings are unique in expression but all are co-equal in Being. I was not more spiritual than others in my world. Minominike was not more spiritual than Adik or Pembina. Lawrence, Pastor Engolf, Peepeelee, James, my current superiors, peers and subordinates are all decreed equals in the family of man, in the eternal now.

The inner frustration of not being allowed the freedom to speak, publish and share fully and openly my experience of this life in the universal Spirit began to mute my conversation with Life itself. Sleep became restless and my level of anger at the institution grew. Soon there was little joy in the routine of liturgy or satisfaction in counseling. The day-to-day logistics of managing a church were drudgery. I often found myself staring yearningly into the distance viewing images of my former northern world. During these mental pictures I would listen to the water on the shore, feel the bite of the wind in the dark season, smell the black spruce and hear it's popping while burning in the stove. I was homesick for the silence and longed for the intimate caress of my Eternal Lover. My life was split between my external role-playing as a 'religious' and the images and desire of my inner world.

My religious world was being shattered. Without a doubt I had loved my system of belief about God more than I had known the Love of God. But now having tasted the limitless envelopment of the ever-present arms of Eternity, seen the subtle enslavement and lies of exclusivist religion and having had the lies of my own ego exposed, I was at the point of decision concerning my future. The arguments that laid the foundation for partitioning the world into accepted or rejected groups warred against the voice in my heart. This interior voice was what drove me to step aside from my indoctrination and that which prevented me from open and honest examination of these divisive assumptions. One by one, invalid central tenants of my exclusivist system continued to be uncovered for the fraud they were. Every time a conflict arose between the voice of my heart and the indoctrination of my mind, it was the later that was in error. Every time. The heart can be trusted. It is the seat of wisdom, the residence of the Spirit of Truth, the Teacher Within. It is the catalyst and source that gently nudges the mind to reexamine what is in conflict with love, unity and peace.

The letters of Minominike regularly and continuously address one central lie, the lie that we are separated from the Great Compassion of the Universe. This lie draws us into its death and the insidious fear of being alone and unloved. Life recedes in apprehension and is filled with false gods as we desperately, in our deception, search to possess that which already possesses us. Love is All in All, the First and the Last, the Beginning and the End. It surrounds and enfolds eternity. We are as much a part of Love as Love is a part of us. Nowhere is this better or more easily seen than in the life, death and resurrection of Minominike's Geezus. He was incarnation of Infinite Love, exposing the lie that grips the mind of man. This universal kingdom of love "is within you" He said. The Spirit of God fills life and we were shown that neither death nor the grave had power to achieve victory over this Love. It ignores the divisions of religion, the races of humankind, the acceptance or rejection of its presence and loves anyway. In the words of Minominike, 'Misiweshkamagad sagiiwe' — all is covered by it.

Where does one begin a list of the deceits our egos wield to hold captive individual lives and the hopes of humankind? Attempting such a list and deconstructing each falsehood would require volumes. At the foundation of each deceit is enthroned the one great lie. Expose this one great lie and the timeless journey into enlightenment, into the security of the Majesty of Eternity, can begin. Drag the one great lie into the Light and our personal reawakening is inevitable. In the words of Mishomis Minominike, "it is for each one to learn." This prophetic phrase was being fulfilled in my heart and I could no longer continue life as usual.

Chapter Eighteen: Returning Home

During this time it was rewarding to see others coming to higher levels of consciousness concerning the truth of our unity in God, creation and humankind. It was satisfying to see my ego and that of others, exposed as the false self it is. Watching others experience the rebirth of their true internal being and begin to uncover its unique value gave me joy.

In the five long years after James' death and my reading of the letters, a radical change and desire had taken place. My spirituality was calling me beyond this particular institution in life. Considering the gag rule that had been imposed on me by the higher authorities that controlled the organization, it was impossible for me to be who I had discovered I was. I resigned.

To reflect, I would say it is a good and right thing to be part of a group, to derive a sense of identity and belonging. It is good to own tradition and ceremony and know its unifying and establishing power. I had lived over three decades in the south. I had developed relationships, built a career and was part of an institution with tradition and ceremony. But now an internal yearning to return to my roots was over-powering; my true identity and belonging could not be ignored. The north was calling. The Ininiwok (people) of my youth, the land, my early history, the Spirit was leading me home.

What I was leaving behind after my resignation had served its purpose. I did not view my years away as wrong or wasted. They were part of my path and had been instrumental in what I now was. Who are we to question the trail our lives take? No matter where the journey has taken us, through truths and deception, the good and the suffering, the ups and downs, the One Who Journeys with Us will use every part in the weaving of a unique soul. We should not, because we cannot, judge the journey when we are incapable of seeing the end. The clay is unqualified to give advice to the Potter or state, "you don't know what you're doing."

Spring arrived. I sold almost everything I owned in the south and purchased a used boat with a small outboard. Up to this point I had flown to Brochet usually once a year to inspect, keep up the cabin and visit friends. For this trip, I loaded my new-used boat with supplies for a simple life in the north and made a slow four-day run up from Southend Indian Reserve located at the opposite terminus of Reindeer Lake. Here and there I met floating rafts of old ice and a few bays were still icebound. From my island camps I watched the earth shadow rise in the east and slept under night skies filled with stars. I recalled the story of Raven bringing the light of the world and spreading it everywhere throughout the great circle of the earth. Under the black sky of new moon, stars gave more than enough light. Each night I whispered "misiweshkamagad sagiiwe," all is covered with it. The Light of the World, the Word, the love of God, shines over all. During the final 30 kilometers, Polaris was more or less directly overhead, Ursa Major keeping an eye as I finally killed the outboard and drifted silently to my shoreline of washed stones. The silence of the north enfolded my being like the Spirit does the universe.

Picking up the canvas bag containing his bundle and the box of letters I stepped out of the boat and draped the bowline over the driftwood root system where kagagi had given me the first feather gift. I stretched to get the kinks out of legs and back, my arm still remembering the vibration brought on by hours at the outboard's tiller. Leaving the other supplies in the boat I labored up the shore. I was home.

The rusty hinges gave an aching creak as the door opened. I decided to leave the boat as it was until morning dawn only a few hours away. After lighting the kerosene lantern on the table and looking around for other life that may have moved in over winter, I inspected the mattress on my old spruce and rope bed and took down some blankets from the shelf. I was weary and looking for sleep. I pulled my head under the covers and caught my warm breath to help drive the chill away.

The next morning my alarm clock was a pair of loons discussing the boat swaying back and forth from its tether to shore. In the ways of this land, I got out my ahsayma (tobacco), a symbol acknowledging His

Presence, my gift of life and my dependency on the Spirit. Raising it in my left hand toward the eastern sky, I gave recognition to the four directions and thanked Grandmother Earth for her beauty and grace in giving us what is needed for life. My heart was settled and I sensed His still small voice speaking peace and tender friendship. From my mouth came the words, "Gi zah gin", I love You.

Postscript—Passing On

It has been several decades since I returned home to Reindeer Lake and penned the words of the previous pages. A new millennium has turned. The small wooden box that held the letters of Minominike now also holds this story of my experience and the revelation the letters initiated in my life. Coming back to the north has been good and richly humbling. I am now old.

I look back and see that in my life I often desired that there was a formula, a recipe to gaining favor and grace with the Great Mystery, but there was no need. Creator Father had given me all the grace and favor needed. There is no searching, just receiving. There is no elite group. We are all special in His sight. There really was no struggle but to cease from my struggling. In this rest I am renewed. In the Presence I am born again each moment. In the Eternal Now, freedom, grace and love surrounds and resides within me. I have never been alone. I can trust in Eternity's kindness. Clearly in life and in death, as shown by that resurrection of long ago, we are never forsaken. Life may be hard to understand, even puzzling. Like Minominike, I, too, often have been at a loss as to its meaning and purpose but this is the privilege of being human. It is what it is. My honor of walking this human journey has been to partake in its joy and pain, wisdom and foolishness, its peace as well as its confusion, the highlights of life and the sorrows of death. My true Being lies completed within and is wrapped in beauty by the sum of all I have experienced. Creator gives the gift of life. What I have done with that gift is my 'megwetch,' my thank you to Him. I believe He replies, "You are welcome." The Great Mystery seems to tell me that all is well.

Many years ago, the year I returned to the north during Waabigwanii Giizis (Flower Moon), I dreamt of the deep black spring Minominike wrote about in his letters. This was the spring given to his grandfathers before him as a sacred place. My father, James, had taken me to it several times after Minominike's passing. Shortly after that dream, I set out to find it after waiting for fall and freeze up in order to make travel easier over wet ground. Not much more than ten-years-old the last time I had been there, I was not sure it could be found again. I knew it was about a day's journey to the north along the Cochrane River and off to the east through dense black spruce. I also remembered walking a long sinuous narrow ridge of land that I have since surmised must have been an esker left by ancient glaciers thousands of years in the past. Within a short distance of the end of this esker, where it rejoined the broader lay of the land, the spring sat surrounded by tamarack, spruce, moss and lichens.

After spending so many years in an urban environment in the south with its unsympathetic lighting, intrusive noise and crush of people, it had taken me awhile to adapt again to the muted glow of long mornings and evenings, the meek sounds of the earth and the open space. This journey in search of the spring was taking me deeper into authentic existence. Apprehensive at first, seemingly all alone on a planet of one, I became even more aware of my Closest Friend.

Many years before, on shorter legs, the distance to the spring would have seemed much more than it actually was. I traveled along the river to what I thought would be the area where James and I would turn away from its banks and head off to the east. Like a spider, I inched my way up a solitary rotund boulder left in millennia past by the ice in order to see over the trees and search for a ridgeline. Most of the forest rarely gets more than several meters high at this latitude. There on the horizon, maybe two kilometers away, was a serpent like ridge slipping into the distance. I smiled about my good fortune, laughed and addressed this geologic oddity with, "nice to see you again." Roughly an hour later I had climbed up the steep side to its sandy crest.

Our relatives of the boreal forest frequently use the tops of eskers as a roadway above the surrounding trees and brush. Its elevation also allows the wind to disperse the insects. Walking this path evoked images of my father's back and legs as I would follow him trying to keep up and trying to step into his tracks on this very ridge. This time I stepped into the tracks of caribou, wolf and bear for over an hour before the ridge came to an abrupt and steeply sloping end. Here, at the edge of world, I lift my face to see, not more than a hundred meters away, the round black, mirrored surface of our spring. I stood amazed considering the generations of life, both human and animal, that stood where I stood, gazing across the beauty and enjoying the Breath of Life.

Visits to the spring of my ancestors, the people who took me in when my birth parents left this world, have been many since that first year of my return north. I am now the age of my father and that of Minominike when they passed on. I meet my people with vivid memories whenever I journey to this sacred space. It has been a place of comfort and sorrow, struggle and peace, a place to quiet the heart and have conversation with the Great Mystery.

Maybe I will be honored to pass through the western door while I am at the spring. Whatever is to come is good. I am finished with writing and will leave this final page on top of the old box containing the letters of Minominike. Maybe others will find the voice of Mishomis Minominike Gissis Makwa opening their heart to the Teacher Within, Our Beloved. There is one world, one family of man, one Father of all. The way of the Spirit is for each person to learn.

Sincerely,
Tulugaq Kagagi   Inabiwin Pindig — Inabiwin Awass Wedi
(Raven Raven)   (Looks Within)   (Looks Beyond)

Anishnabe Word Locator

All words are from the Anishnabe language unless otherwise noted to be Inuktitut, Dakota or Hebrew.

Word	Letter Number
Ahmek (beaver)	13; 22; 26
Ahnung (star)	35
Anishnabe (original people)	27; 28; 29; 30
Ashayma (tobacco)	19; 28; 30; 31; 36; 40
Asabikeshii (spider)	22
Asub (net)	23
Ba Wa Ting (water tumbling over rocks)	28; 30
Banayshee (bird)	22; 34
Banaysheug (birds)	22
Bawazigaywin (dream)	6; 39
Beboong (winter)	42
Binoojiing (child)	28
Bizhiw (lynx)	16; 40
Chi Megwetch (thank you very much)	30
Chi Wajiwan (big mountain)	36
Daniye'l (Daniel — Hebrew)	14
Dende (bullfrog)	7; 16; 22; 35; 36; 41
Gawg (porcupine)	31; 40
Geezus (Jesus)	12; 14; 15; 22; 26; 38; 40; 42
Gi zah gin (I love you)	38
Gichi Gami (great lake, Lake Superior)	28; 30
Gichi Ka Be Kong (great falls, Niagara Falls)	28; 30
Gichi Manidoo (Great Spirit)	14; 15; 17; 23; 28-31; 34; 36; 38; 40; 42
Gichi Sabi (great man of the forest)	12; 13; 22; 26
Giigoonh (fish)	18
Giigoonh Ahsubbi (fish net)	32
Giizis (moon)	22
Gishkibidagunnun (bundle)	31

Synopsis of Letters

Onaabani Giizis

Letter One

1—Ode'imini Giizis 1931

(Time for Picking Berries Moon)

Minominike introduces himself and talks of Adik, James and Peepeelee. He mentions the circumstances by which Tulugaq Kagagi came to them and hints at the teaching of the Great Giveaway. Grandmother Adik also speaks about picking berries.

Letter Two

2—Ode'imini Giizis 1931

(Time for Picking Berries Moon)

Minominike tells his story of Raven redeeming the world from darkness.

Letter Three

Aabita Niibino Giizis 1931

(Halfway Through Summer Moon)

Minominike explains the story of Raven redeeming the world from darkness. Grandmother Adik also speaks of catching and eating Namegossika (trout).

Letter Four

Manoominike Giizis 1931

(Rice Gathering Moon)

Recounting of the story of Makwa (bear) falling into the river. Minominike tells about his young life and time at school. He describes his inner conflict on hearing about the partiality of God's love and explains the difference between the words of the world and the words of the Spirit in our heart. He tells the story of the Wewe (goose) "downy feather" speaking to him to return north, leaving school behind, and explains that none are ever left out in the cold by God. He talks briefly about his marrying Adik.

Letter Five

1—Waatebagaa Giizis 1931

(Leaves Changing Color Moon)

The teaching of the four directions and the understanding that the Great Mystery possesses both male and female characteristics yet is not a human.

Letter Six

2—Waatebagaa Giizis 1931

(Leaves Changing Color Moon)

Minominike tells of his dream while sleeping under his canoe—darkness is unable to overcome light.

Letter Seven

3—Waatebagaa Giizis 1931

(Leaves Changing Color Moon)

The teaching of our world's unity and oneness as illustrated by the one source of all the stones of Reindeer Lake. Minominike ties this teaching into the toy carvings he has made from the same one source, the spruce tree.

Letter Eight

1—Binaakwii Giizis 1931

(Falling Leaves Moon)

Minominike uses an analogy of a string connecting all people to the heart of God. He speaks of love as the beginning and ending of all things and the relationship of love with the "giveaway." He gives examples in creation while speaking to the need for human beings to seek the attitude of 'giveaway' in our own hearts. He states that 'giveaway' is the greatest teaching and that the universe is ultimately benevolent.

Letter Nine

2—Binaakwii Giizis 1931

(Falling Leaves Moon)

A short allegory dealing with the equality of all people as illustrated by leaves on a tree.

Letter Ten

3—Binaakwii Giizis 1931

(Falling Leaves Moon)

A young moose gives itself to Minominike and Adik for food. He discusses the privilege of walking our human journey and discovering our uniqueness while the journey of our relations, the animals, is a path already revealed within them. Through the illustration of nakedness he goes on to describe how shame and fear fill our lives and freedom is lost. Humor ends the letter with "the noise of the beans."

Letter Eleven

1—Gashkadino Giizis 1931

(Ice is Forming Moon)

The bear visits Tulugaq Kagagi's cabin at night. Adik's heart attack.

Letter Twelve

2—Gashkadino Giizis 1931

(Ice is Forming Moon)

First four teachings out of seven: Maiingan (wolf), Makwa (bear), Kinew (eagle) and Gichi Sabe (great man of the forest).

Letter Thirteen

3—Gashkadino Giizis 1931

(Ice is Forming Moon)

Last three teachings out of seven: Ahmek (beaver), Mashkode Biziki (bison) and Mikinaak (turtle).

Letter Fourteen

Manidoo Giizisoons 1931

(Little Spirit Moon)

Names of the Creator and explanation of the Incarnation.

Letter Fifteen

Gichi Manidoo Giizis 1932

(Great Spirit Moon)

Minominike's teaching of how the world is filled with wars and division because human beings do not know the unity of the Spirit. He talks of WWI and mentions the Civil War. He continues with the story of his experience catching the great Namegossika (trout) and how this is a picture of the reality of God's love whether we can see it or not.

Letter Sixteen

Namebini Giizis 1932

(Sucker Moon)

Story of Dende fighting the Bizhiw (lynx). Mishomis Minominike tells about fighting the red-haired Scottish boy and how this is an example of what happens when we are not led by the Spirit.

Letter Seventeen

1—Onaabani Giizis 1932

(Hard Crust on Snow Moon)

First mention of Father Engolf. Prediction that Tulugaq Kagagi may one day be taught things contrary to the whispers of his heart. In spite of religion's claim to speak for God, God can speak for Himself.

Letter Eighteen

2—Onaabani Giizis 1932

(Hard Crust on Snow Moon)

Mishomis Minominike tells about the meaning of the name Tulugaq Kagagi and also that someday a new name would be given to him, Inabiwin Pindig — Inabiwin Awass Wedi.

Letter Nineteen

Iskigamizige Giizis 1932

(Maple Sugar Moon)

The prayer of Minominike as he greets each day.

Letter Twenty

1—Waabigwanii Giizis 1932

(Flower Moon)

Willie loses his toes. The progressive teaching about the struggle to be somebody, to thinking we are nobody, to seeing we are everybody.

Letter Twenty-One

2—Waabigwanii Giizis 1932

(Flower Moon)

Minominike discusses the peril of being given too many answers before we ask the questions.

Letter Twenty-Two

3—Waabigwanii Giizis 1932

(Flower Moon)

Five observations of the difference between the ways of the south and the ways of the Anishnabe.

1— The way of unity and respect.

2 — The way of watching for the sacred.

3 — The way of freedom.

4 — The way of restoration.

5 — The way of community and family. Adik tells of her history with Minominike.

Letter Twenty-Three

Ode'imini giizis 1932

(Time for Picking Berries Moon)

The story of Pembina's near drowning and how this experience taught him not to struggle against life but let the arms of the Creator carry him when times are hard. Minominike also tells about the deaths of Albert and Angeni and how this caused him to grieve nearly to the point of his own dying. He shares his encounter with the Black Makwa at the sacred spring of his fathers and how this time brought comfort in his time of grief.

Letter Twenty-Four

Aabita niibino giizis 1932

(Halfway Through Summer Moon)

The prayer made during the time of morning for Albert and Angeni.

Letter Twenty-Five

1—Manoominike giizis 1932

(Rice Gathering Moon)

Father Engolf, Tulugaq Kagagi and Minominike watch the ravens torment a moose by the sandbar in the river.

Letter Twenty-Six

2—Manoominike giizis 1932

(Rice Gathering Moon)

An explanation on how the teachings of Maiingan (wolf), Makwa (bear), Kinew (eagle), Gichi Sabe (great man of the forest), Ahmek (beaver), Mashkode Biziki (bison) and Mikinaak (turtle) are also embodied in Jesus.

Letter Twenty-Seven

1—Waatebagaa Giizis 1932

(Leaves Changing Color Moon)

The story of the little boy Wiin Wanendan (He Forgets) and his little sister Wiin Mikwinan (She Remembers). This begins Minominike's mystical teachings of the journey of life.

Letter Twenty-Eight

2—Waatebagaa Giizis 1932

(Leaves Changing Color Moon)

Minominike recounts the prophecies of the Seven Fires and the historical journey of the Anishnabe from the eastern end of the St. Lawrence River to the Great Lakes and beyond.

Letter Twenty-Nine

3—Waatebagaa Giizis 1932

(Leaves Changing Color Moon)

Minominike begins to explain the prophecies of the Seven Fires and the historical journey of the Anishnabe as a parable showing us the steps intended for our journey of life.

Letter Thirty

4—Waatebagaa Giizis 1932

(Leaves Changing Color Moon)

He continues to unravel the 'stopping places' of the Seven Fires prophecy. He explains the stages of awareness or levels of consciousness in our life journey that bring us to greater freedom and security in the benevolence of the Creator. The letter ends with his prayer seeking Tulugaq Kagagi's understanding.

Letter Thirty-One

Binaakwii Giizis 1932

(Falling Leaves Moon)

The description of Minominike's sacred bundle and the items it contains. He talks about each item and how it is used in his personal ceremony to help center his mind on spiritual things. He also writes his prayers used in his ceremony. Adik's recounting of the stones and quill box she has made for Tulugaq Kagagi.

Letter Thirty-Two

1—Gashkadino Giizis 1932

(Ice is Forming Moon)

Nokomis Adik tells the story of how she created a charm to draw Minominike to love her. Minominike describes his sweat lodge ceremony. Two ravens laugh at him for writing so much.

Letter Thirty-Three

2—Gashkadino Giizis 1932

(Ice is Forming Moon)

This letter contains the beginning of a series of stories about mystical spiritual happenings in Minominike's life.

Letter Thirty-Four

3—Gashkadino Giizis 1932

(Ice is Forming Moon)

Minominike continues his stories about his mystical experiences. Adik comments about her vision/revelation of the Creator possessing attributes of both man and woman.

Letter Thirty-Five

Manidoo giizisoons 1932

(Little Spirit Moon)

It was recently Tulugaq Kagagi's fifth birthday. Minominike talks about his looking through binoculars. He is seeing into the future and believes more of the family of man will begin to renew their minds to the truth of the world's oneness. He also describes the path of life as a walk in the woods. It is hardly ever in a straight line. If we get lost at night we need to find our star and it will lead us to our destination.

Letter Thirty-Six

Waabigwanii giizis 1933

(Flower Moon)

The letter telling of Adik's death.

Letter Thirty-Seven

1—Aabita niibino giizis 1933

(Halfway Through Summer Moon)

Lawrence visits Minominike in his time of loneliness. Mishomis talks about the "skin of the spirit."

Letter Thirty-Eight

2—Aabita niibino giizis 1933

(Halfway Through Summer Moon)

Lawrence writes his letter to Tulugaq Kagagi.

Letter Thirty-Nine

Manoominike giizis 1933

(Rice Gathering Moon)

Minominike tells about the swimming accident and his dream of a large garden.

Letter Forty

1—Binaakwii Giizis 1933

(Falling Leaves Moon)

Minominike visits the sacred spring and again sees the Great Black Makwa. He discusses looking at other people through the eyes of Gichi Manidoo and describes for Tulugaq Kagagi the amazing column of fog that rose from the spring.

Letter Forty-One

1—Binaakwii Giizis 1933

(Falling Leaves Moon)

Grandfather says he will carve an airplane for Tulugaq Kagagi's sixth birthday, which will be coming up in another moon.

Letter Forty-Two

Gichi Manidoo Giizis 1934

(Great Spirit Moon)

It is winter and Minominike sees his breath as a picture of life. He pens a prayer for his white grandson to know his name is Inabiwin Pindig—Inabiwin Awass Wedi (Looks Within—Looks Beyond)

Letter Forty-Three

Iskigamizige Giizis 1934

(Maple Sugar Moon)

The farewell letter.

About the Author

James "Pep" Washburn was born and raised in rural Wisconsin, initiating an intimate rapport with the natural environment and life in the north. Drawing from his connections to native North American Indian and Inuit people, as well as a deep personal spiritual history in traditional Christianity, he weaves a story that transcends religion, ethnicity and culture. He speaks to the universal desires of the human heart with simplicity and passion. He is involved in advocating for peace and reconciliation in our world.

Washburn attended the University of Wisconsin — Stevens Point. He was a teacher/librarian for thirty-three years and nominated for Wisconsin State Teacher of the Year in 1983. He is married, has two adult children, and is an avid hiker-explorer.

Cover Photo by Edward S. Curtis; *Agoyo-tsa (Star White)*
Charles Deering McCormick Library of Special Collections,
Northwestern University Library, Evanston, Illinois

48580087R00208

Made in the USA
Lexington, KY
05 January 2016